THE CRAB BOYS

THE CRAB BOYS

Nancy Rhyne

SANDLAPPER PUBLISHING CO., INC.
ORANGEBURG, SOUTH CAROLINA

FIRST EDITION

Published by Sandlapper Publishing Co., Inc.
Orangeburg, South Carolina

Manufactured in the United States of America

Library of Congress Cataloging-in-Publication Data

Rhyne, Nancy, 1926–
The crab boys / Nancy Rhyne. — 1st ed.
p. cm.
Summary: Rhett and Gaffney, aged ten and eleven, find adventure crabbing, fishing, and searching for sunken treasure in South Carolina's Low Country in 1947.
ISBN 978-0-87844-183-9 (pbk. : alk. paper)
[1. Adventure and adventurers—Fiction. 2. Crabbing—Fiction. 3. Fishing—Fiction. 4. Buried treasure—Fiction. 5. South Carolina—History—20th century—Fiction.] I. Title.

PZ7.R3479Cra 2007
[Fic]—dc22

2007020806

AUTHOR'S NOTE

Rhett Gingyard and Gaffney Dorn, the leading characters in this book, are fictional. The events and crises in their lives, however, happened to people in the South Carolina Low Country. The fearful incidents are very real, and they came to me while doing research in the WPA narratives in September 2005 at the South Caroliniana Library, University of South Carolina, Columbia, South Carolina. I would not have found these tales without the assistance of the library's director, Herbert J. Hartsook, and members of his staff, Henry Fulmer, Graham Duncan, Beth Bildeback, Brian Cuthrell, Robin Copp, Beverly Bullock, and Ashley Bowden. I also owe a great debt of thanks to coastal South Carolina residents who told me stories that appear in this book, such as the visits of Gen. George Marshall and the lesson learned from his experiences. As I thank those who made this book possible, Barbara Stone, my superb editor, leads the way. Not only is her excellent editing of vast importance, but I am thankful for her friendship as well. I am also grateful for Amanda Gallman whose steady hand moves the wheel at Sandlapper Publishing. My husband Sid, more than anyone else, remains supportive and reassuring during the long hours spent at the computer. To him, my life's partner and biggest fan, I owe a lifetime of thanks.

Nancy Rhyne
Columbia, South Carolina

About our Main Characters

Rhett Gingyard and Gaffney Dorn live on The Barony. Rhett's father serves as superintendent and Gaff's father as game warden. This story takes place around 1947. Talk of the atomic bomb is big news across the country. Rhett and Gaff are busy with their adventures and not concerned much about wars in foreign lands. There is plenty of action on The Barony to keep them occupied. Rhett is the younger of the two, just by a year. He's ten. His thick dark hair shows off pale blue eyes, inherited from his dad. Eleven-year-old Gaff is tall for his age—about five-foot-ten—and towers a bit over his friend. His fair hair is almost white in the summer, which makes his bright green eyes—like those of his mom—seem even brighter. Gaff's more serious nature complements Rhett's carefree, I'll-try-anything-once attitude. They watch each other's back, and rather than helping to keep each other out of trouble, they dive in headfirst together. Life along the South Carolina coast offers an abundance of wildlife and activities. Our two young suntanned protagaonists offer us an entertaining glimpse into the lives of southern youth in post-World War II Carolina.

THE CRAB BOYS

CHAPTER ONE

The Crab Boys

"My dad says The Barony mudflats and oyster banks are a temptation luring us to a dangerous ocean," Rhett Gingyard said to his friend Gaffney Dorn, as they carried their buckets toward the oyster banks.

Gaffney carefully placed each foot on a steady piece of grassy mud as the boys picked their way through the half-land, half-water salt marsh. "Heck," he said, "what does he think we'll do, swim out to the lighthouse on North Island?"

"He knows *we* know better than to do something like that. Dad spends lots of time considering all the creatures under the surface of the sea. The ocean's deep out there. He says there are old ships lying on the bottom of Winyah Bay. They make perfect reefs for the sea monsters."

"Sea monsters?"

Rhett pointed to the ocean beyond the marsh and oyster banks. "Plenty of 'em. Right out there."

"Such as?" Gaffney asked.

Rhett stopped. "What about the spider-shaped octopus with the large head or the shark with dozens of teeth? And even the stone crabs that spread their jagged claws—like the ones we'll take from their deep holes today." He swung his empty bucket out for his friend to see.

"Listen, Rhett, I'll bet your dad eats his share of the crab meat on the supper table."

"Boy, does he! But he always tells me to be careful and twist off the big claw, drop it in the bucket, and throw the rest of the critter back into the briny. Crabs retread themselves, you know."

"Like automobile tires?"

"Stone crabs do," Rhett said.

"Stone crabs have that big claw with the good crab meat." Gaff licked his lips. "The other claws grow bigger after that big one with the best meat is gone."

"Yeah, who knows how many times we've taken the same stone crab we ate on the year before?"

"Well, all I care about is filling my bucket," Gaff said. "Mama's counting on a good supper."

Rhett nodded his head. "Get the row boat," he called out.

Gaffney pulled a small boat from a clump of bushes. The boys carried the vessel to the inlet and climbed aboard. They each took an oar from the bottom and began rowing. The inlet, a lagoon, ran along the side of the marshland. It emptied into Winyah Bay at the Atlantic Ocean, not far from the mudflats and oyster banks. As Rhett and Gaff paddled for deeper water, they saw a familiar boat moving toward them from the sea.

"Mornin'," the man called. "How're the crab boys faring this mornin'?"

"Fine," Gaff yelled in response. After the boats had traveled some distance away from each other, he asked Rhett, "Why do you think he always calls us 'the crab boys'?"

"For one thing," Rhett said, "everybody else calls us that. We're boys—I'm ten and you're almost twelve—and we furnish the crab meat for our families' supper. Nobody gets as many stone crabs as we do."

"Most folks bring in blue crabs, but not us," Gaff added. "We're brave enough to go for the good stuff."

"Getting blue crabs is easier and safer," Rhett agreed. "They're everywhere. And besides, blue crabs don't have that huge claw that's just waiting to snap shut on our hands and break our fingers and hold us captive until the tide comes in and the water rises over our heads."

"Don't even talk about that," Gaff growled. "You sound like your dad. He's forever talking about safety in crabbing."

"He does that all right. All the living, daylight time. But he's right, you know. There's a lot of danger in getting a stone crab. That's why not many people do it. Dad doesn't want us to have anything to do with danger. It's his job to keep everybody safe

and everything in good condition on this place. That's why he's the superintendent of The Barony. Mr. Blackhall counts on him to run a safe operation. Dad doesn't intend for any accidents to happen. Being the superintendent of The Barony isn't just any old job."

"I've heard my dad say it's a big responsibility. The superintendent is the paymaster, the yachtsman, the dog minder, the horse minder, and the hunting guide."

"And that's not all," Rhett said. "He's the mechanic and the plumber. He takes care of the electrics, and he's the doctor when somebody gets sick."

Gaff looked a little downtrodden. He wasn't sure his dad's status as game warden at The Barony was as important as Rhett's dad's. "My mom's the cook for Mr. Blackhall's famous visitors from Washington, such as the general," he offered.

"Your mom is the best cook in the world," Rhett said. "You get to eat at the big house a lot and I don't get to do that. Your dad's job is as high as my dad's. Mr. Blackhall tells everybody how lucky he is to have the game warden living on his property. Mr. Blackhall spends more time with your dad than he does with mine."

"That's because Mr. Blackhall doesn't allow any poachers on this land. He hates poachers, and Dad hauls them right to jail." Gaff said, as he continued to row.

"Why *does* Mr. Blackhall dislike poachers so much? He shudders if anyone mentions the word *poacher.*"

"They sneak onto his land and hide 'till the coast is clear. They take alligators and sell the hide, and they kill deer for food."

"What does your dad do to the poachers?"

"He gives them a piece of his mind and then escorts them to jail," Gaff said with pride. "I can tell Mr. Blackhall admires my dad. He's different from most of the other men around here. He doesn't laugh with the other men and tell jokes. Mama says he carries the weight of The Barony on his shoulders. Mr. Blackhall says he got a bargain when he got the game warden and that's why we get our house free, like you do."

"I've heard Mr. Blackhall say he's happy your dad lives on The Barony. And your mom too. She sure does cook good."

"Mom's cooking supper right now for General George Marshall. Dad and I will eat the same food, but not at the table with the general and Mr. and Mrs. Blackhall. Mom's making her special she crab soup and she told me to bring any crab claws I get to the kitchen. She'll add the crab meat to the soup." Gaff rememberd the boatman they passed. "We'll do that because we're 'the crab boys'," he added, grinning.

"Hey, maybe we could make a song out of that," Rhett said. In his best country singer imitation, he sang, "The crab boys of Georgetown County, South Carolina, in the summer of 1947."

"Sing on, Crab Boy," Gaff encouraged.

"The crab boys! The crab boys! They get their crabs and make no noise," Rhett continued.

The boys dissolved into laughter.

CHAPTER TWO

The Oyster Banks

"Looka. See the oyster banks and the holes the stone crabs dug in between the oyster shells and the big rocks?" Rhett pointed to the bank, a manmade embankment built to prevent flooding. Covered in oyster shells, it was popularly called the oyster banks. "Those crab holes go down deep, and I mean *deep*. The ole stone crab is just a-sitting down there in the pluff mud, thinking nothing's going to happen to him."

"I see the folks from Clam Cove," Gaff said, using his hands as a visor against the sun. "There's Abraham and his grandson Welcome."

"They get their oysters here every day," Rhett said. He craned his neck. "I think there's an unfamiliar boat down there in the shallows. Look."

Gaff and Rhett pushed their rowboat onto the oyster banks and walked the rest of the way to the crab holes.

"Hey, Abraham," Rhett called. "What's up?"

"Lost my wife," Abraham said.

"You lost your wife?" Rhett asked.

"Death come in and make alterations," Abraham

answered. "Hard living make contrivance. She'd take any old coat, or anything, and take it apart and make it over to fit the chillun. If you saw our chillun on the street, they were turned out. All our chillun was girls 'cept one boy, Welcome."

"I'm sorry to hear that, Mr. Abe," Gaff called out.

"Hard living without her," the old man said.

The three stood quiet for a few minutes, then Rhett said, "I think there's a strange boat in the distance."

"I don't see no boat," Abraham answered.

"Follow me, Gaff."

A sandy path at the top of the long oyster bank extended to Winyah Bay, to the "dangerous ocean" that worried Rhett's dad. The boys followed the path until they saw a boat bobbing in the waves, near the shore. "That's not a Barony boat," Gaff said. "And where are the people?"

Rhett looked at the huge expanse of dark gray-blue ocean. White caps exploded near the shoreline.

"Where are the people, you reckon?" Gaff asked again.

"I don't know," Rhett replied, "but if they think they can get some of the stone crabs, they're in for a surprise. You have to know the secret of getting those suckers out of the hole, or a crab'll do what it always does, get your hand and hold it 'till judgment day."

"You're right about that," Gaff said. "It happened

to Bryan and he's in the graveyard over at Mount Moriah."

"That tide comes in real fast and stone crabs don't have a habit of turning loose when they take hold," Rhett said.

"Dad said he knows a family who lost several children that way."

"My dad knows them too. That's why he preaches day and night, 'use a wire with a hook on the end'."

"Like the grown-ups use?"

Rhett nodded. "One and the same. They slowly work the wire down into the hole and hook the crab before he knows what's going on. They don't put their hands near the crab."

"Why should we use a wire with a hook?" Gaff

asked, rolling his eyes. "Just because the grown folks do? Heck no. Our arms are the exact length of the crabs' holes. We know how to hold our hand rigid and press the outside of it against the sidewall as we reach down into the hole the crab digs among the oyster shells."

"You've got to remember though that old lobster-like, flat-bodied crustacean with his eyes on stalks knows the hand is there," Rhett cautioned. "He's just waiting for the right time to grab it and he'll hold onto it 'till doomsday."

"Yeah," Gaff agreed. "Too many have died to question that."

"I don't want to be in the cemetery at Mount Moriah anytime soon." Rhett shuddered. "But we know what we're doing, and I don't care if Dad tells me a million or more times that our method and scheme may not always work. I believe it will."

Gaff looked at the ocean. "Tide's coming in. We better get to the crab holes while the water level is still low."

"Wait a minute," Rhett whispered. He noticed a couple walking near the oyster bank. They turned and headed back to the strange boat. "I think we're rid of the boat people."

"We know the folks from Clam Cove," Gaff said. "Their families have lived on The Barony for generations. Those folks aren't from around here. . . . Well, they're leaving. Let's go fill our buckets."

Rhett was the first to reach down the crab's hole. His bucket sat nearby. He stiffened his hand and arm and lowered them slowly into the short tunnel. "I can almost see the old crab now," he said to Gaff, "sitting so straight, all propped up and holding that big claw up in front of those bug eyes, ready to make his move. But I'm smarter than he is. WOWEE." Rhett suddenly yanked his hand up and pulled out pluff mud and stone crab. He tossed his bounty over his head. He rose quickly and walked to the crab. The stone crab moved his claw slightly in an effort to escape his captor. Rhett placed a thumb under the shell of the crab and his forefinger on the top and lifted the creature up. He took a rag from his pocket and used it to twist off the large claw. As he dropped the claw into his bucket, he clucked through his teeth, indicating his accomplishment. In the style of his favorite professional baseball pitcher, he threw the crab in a high arc that curved over the oyster banks and landed in the inlet.

"Got him!" Gaff yelled as he pulled out *his* first crab of the day. Like Rhett, he twisted off the large claw, dropped it into his bucket, and pitched the crab into the water.

When their crab buckets were full, Rhett asked, "Want to get some oysters? There're plenty big and juicy ones in the shells on the oyster banks"

"My dad brought in a basket of oysters yesterday," Gaff answered. "The general loves steamed oysters and Dad's helping my mom get them ready for supper tonight."

"Come on," Rhett said, heading toward the little boat in the bushes. He peered into Gaff's bucket. "We got a good catch of crabs. The general can stuff his face on that crab meat in your bucket."

The boys put their buckets into the boat, placed the oars in the bottom, and were soon back at the shady area where they kept their boat hidden in the foliage. They pushed it into the bushes where no eye could detect it. Holding tightly to their heavy buckets they didn't walk home the usual way. Gaff planned to deliver his crab claws to his mother at the big house. After they came across the marsh area they eyed The Barony landing. A pier jutted into Winyah Bay on the far side of the mansion. Several of Mr. Blackhall's big boats rode at anchor there.

"Have you ever ridden in one of those boats?" Rhett asked.

"What boats?"

"*The Cat's Tail, The Puppy Love,* and *The Tide's Up*—Mr. Blackhall's vessels."

"No," Gaff said as he veered away from his friend and walked toward a hill leading to the big, white-pillared house. "See ya."

Gaff presented his mother with the gift of stone crab claws. She hugged him and told him to come back for supper and she would let him see an honest-to-goodness United States general, statesman, and secretary of state, George C. Marshall.

Rhett walked on toward his family's home near the estate's entrance gate. When he gave his bounty to his mother she told him that Mrs. Dorn had invited him to join Gaffney and his family for dinner in the pantry, where they could listen in on conversations with General Marshall.

"All right!" Rhett yelled.

He was excited about eating at the big house and listening to General Marshall. He wanted to remember all he could of what this important man had to say. Gaff would make sure he got a glimpse of the famous guest.

Mr. Gingyard looked at the crab claws in the bucket and asked if anything unusual had happened. Rhett told him a boat and a couple visitors he didn't recognize had anchored in the inlet but left quickly. After warning his son that bad weather was predicted for the following day, he cautioned, "Don't even entertain the thought of going crabbing. You know how boisterous the tide can get, not to mention how edgy the crabs are in stormy weather."

Rhett really didn't need his dad's warning. The boys' plans for the next day had already been made. A little rough weather wasn't anything they couldn't handle.

CHAPTER THREE

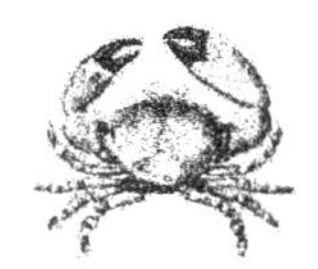

The General

"Rhett, you may sit here, next to Gaffney and his father," Mrs. Dorn said. "Listen carefully now. The people who will dine in the dining room do not know you are here. I'm counting on all of you to behave mighty fine, nice and quiet."

"We can handle that," Mr. Dorn responded. "Has the general been seated?"

Mrs. Dorn glanced out the pantry door. "No." She put a finger over her lips. "Shh. I'll get your supper," she whispered.

When Mrs. Dorn returned, she carried a large, white platter. The right side was piled high with fried chicken. Green beans filled the center, and a mound of potato salad balanced the other side. She stuck a large spoon into the potato salad. Soundlessly, she served each plate with a generous helping of each offering. Using her hands, she dropped several cubes of ice from a bowl into glasses of sweet tea. "Not much of this," she whispered. "I don't want to hear any tinkling of ice—or whispering."

"Yes, ma'am," Gaff mouthed in response.

Nearly half an hour passed before the general

was ushered into the dining room. Mrs. Dorn stuck her head into the pantry and was happy to see that her husband, Gaff, and Rhett had already consumed their supper. They sat quietly, waiting.

Mr. and Mrs. Blackhall and the general were seated and served. For awhile, they chatted about inconsequential things. Then Mr. Blackhall asked the general, "What do you think about the atomic bomb?"

"It's a matter that has to be dealt with," General Marshall answered. "Like the hurricanes that you expect to beat a path to your house, you have to prepare, take precautions, use all preventive measures at your disposal."

"The hurricanes are an act of God. There is no way to stop them," Mr. Blackhall said. "The bomb is a threat of our own design—the outcome disastrous."

"We're all afraid, of course we are. It was just about one year ago, on a dark and dreary night, that Robert Oppenheimer made his way onto a stage in a secret location—Los Alamos, New Mexico—and announced to an audience of scientists that they who had fashioned the first atomic bombs with their own hands had brought to an end the most destructive war in human history."

"It could be that their bomb will *start* the most horrendous war in human history," Mr. Blackhall countered. "I cannot imagine the scientists believed any positive benefit would result from their bomb, and it is beyond me to fathom what Oppenheimer was thinking. Who's in charge of the bomb?"

"What do you mean?" the general asked.

"Who has the authority to say, 'Drop the bomb' or 'The Bomb shall not be used at this time'?"

"I do," General Marshall answered calmly.

"You? Only you?" Mr. Blackhall all but screamed.

"Only me. I am in charge of the bomb."

"Millions of innocent lives will be lost if the bomb is used," Mr. Blackhall spat with contempt. "Whole countries will disappear from the earth. Who gave you such immense control?"

"President Truman."

Mr. Dorn chose a moment when Mr. Blackhall was shouting to gaze at Rhett and Gaff. They were taking it all in. "This is history," Mr. Dorn murmured under his breath. "Listen to every word. We'll discuss it later."

"I spoke to the United Nations last week," Mr. Blackhall was saying. "I told the members of the Atomic Energy Commission that behind the black portent of the new Atomic Age lies a hope that, seized upon with faith, can work out salvation. If we fail, then we have damned every man to be the slave of fear. Let us not deceive ourselves; we must elect world peace or world destruction."

"I heard your speech and I have a plan," the general answered. "More than one plan, as a matter of fact."

"Do you care to discuss them with me?" Mr. Blackhall asked.

"Only one of them, and this is not the appropriate time."

"Francie! Bring the coffee!" Mr. Blackhall shouted to Mrs. Dorn. It was clear he believed the atomic bomb could bring the world to its knees. And one man had the authority to make that happen—General George Marshall."

Gaff and his father accompanied Rhett home. As they walked along, they talked about the general and all he had said.

"Do you think someone will drop the bomb on us?" Rhett asked.

Mr. Dorn surveyed the sky before he answered. "No. This is what I think: you and Gaffney are safe at The Barony, safer than most people in the country. You can go about your business quite unburdened of worry. But I am concerned about you getting into trouble. You boys have this rich and vast place in which to enjoy all the pleasures of nature. If you are not careful, something dreadful could happen. Our government provides us with a large degree of happiness and safety, but if we do not manage it adequately, control it thoroughly, we will face danger."

"I'm careful, Daddy," Gaff said. "Don't worry

about me."

"Nor me," Rhett added. "You're the game warden and you know everything about this land."

"No, I don't know everything." Mr. Dorn smiled.

"I think you know everything," Rhett said. "Are there some vessels lying on the bottom of the sea where the inlet goes into Winyah Bay?"

"Years ago, there was a war fought here, the Civil War, only it wasn't very civil. Brother fought against brother, cousin against cousin. The only good thing to result was the abolishment of the system of slavery. No person can be held a slave in this country, and that's good."

"But the vessels on the bottom of the sea?" Rhett reminded.

"During that war the federal government threw up a blockade in Charleston Harbor. The people of Charleston had no medicines; the women had no cloth; there was no tea except the sassafras tea made from roots and barks. Some enterprising men fashioned slim vessels that could escape the blockade by going in and out of the harbor at midnight or during a storm. They brought items the Charlestonians needed. Many of the pilots chose inlets from which to deal in their business, lagoons such as Big Mouth Inlet, the one that empties into Winyah Bay. Almost every inlet on this coast serves as a cemetery to blockade running ships. The resourceful men, the blockade runners, made lots of money, millions of dollars in Confederate gold, but most of the pilots didn't live to enjoy it. The larger ships overtook them and today they lie on the bottom of the sea. There are people who believe the inlets are paved with gold."

"Really?" Rhett was dumbfounded.

"Oh, I expect there are some blockade runners on the bottom of the inlet, but what ever is there must lie in its grave. Don't give a thought to violating anything lying at the bottom of the sea. That's the largest graveyard in the world."

If it hadn't been as dark as midnight, Gaff would have seen the hangdog look Rhett gave him.

CHAPTER FOUR

"Do we dare?"

Dawn blew in fiercely next morning, bending the palmetto trees nearly to the ground. Still, after breakfast, Rhett and Gaff braced the wind and carried their buckets through the marsh.

"My dad warned against bad weather," Rhett said.

"I hope he doesn't come looking for us."

"I don't think he will," Rhett answered. "He has a big job today. Mr. Blackhall wants some of the cypress trees taken out of the Danseuse Drifts area. He's planning a party over there for some Washington politicians and intends to have a big barbecue."

"Are they having a deer drive?"

"Sure. The guests usually stay overnight in the old mansion on the dunes. They can hunt at night, which is their favorite time. The deer come out to the sand drifts, which are white as snow on a night that's especially bright. It's a sight to see—the deer running around the high drifts. That's one of Mr. Blackhall's favorite entertainments—giving hunting parties for senators and congressmen from Washington. They're invited to stay a couple nights at

Danseuse Drifts to hunt deer, and then they end the outing with a bountiful barbecue on the beach."

"Who cooks the barbecue?" Gaff wanted to know. His mother, who cooked for most Barony occasions, had never mentioned such an event.

"Splitfoot Honeycutt. He's the flat-out number-one best barbecue cooker in existence. Mr. Blackhall has the best time of all. After a deer drive, if any-one shot at a deer and failed to bring him down, Mr. Blackhall cuts off a piece of that hunter's shirt. Mr. Blackhall has a big flag made of those pieces of shirt. It waves over the entrance to Danseuse Drifts Manor."

"Do the hunters object to their shirts being cut?" Gaff asked.

"Heck, yeah! Dad says some of them wear new shirts, and they ride the horses fast to get away from Mr. Blackhall. But he's deadset on getting a piece of their shirt tail."

"What does Mr. Blackhall intend to do with the cypress trees?"

"He'll probably make paneling out of them. All the paneling in Blackhall Manor is of cypress," Rhett explained. "Dad said he hoped there'll be enough left over for him to make a table for our porch."

"Your dad's definitely busy today, so he won't be looking for us," Gaff concluded.

"That's for sure. What about your dad?"

Gaff thought a minute and said, "He's lying in

wait for some poachers in the deer park."

"Where's the deer park? I never heard of it."

"You ever ride after dark on the road that leads from the gate to Blackhall Manor?"

"Too many times to count," Rhett answered.

"If you go there at night and shine the car lights into the trees, you'll see a million tiny lights, just like at Christmas. Only they're not lights, they're the eyes of the deer in that region. My dad calls the entrance road the deer park."

"Why is he expecting poachers?"

"He's heard some talk. Almost every night he gets his gun and walks in that direction."

"Well, why is he looking for poachers in broad daylight?" Rhett asked.

"He's not looking for them now. He's piling up some fallen trees into a sort of deer blind, like the

hunters use on a deer drive. Only this time Dad'll be waiting for poachers and not deer."

"Then, he won't be looking for us either," Rhett said.

"Not as long as the daylight lasts."

"Say, Gaff. What do you say we take a look at the inlet where it shakes hands with the Atlantic Ocean—you know, where the blockade running boats sank?"

A gust of wind almost blew Gaff off his feet. He recovered and looked hard at his friend. "In this weather?"

"There isn't any weather under the water. We might have a look."

"You mean you think we should go down to the bottom of the sea?" Gaff asked.

"No. You crazy? I mean just below the surface, far enough to see the carcass of a blockade runner on the bottom. We might find a fortune in gold. It's been said that every blockade runner that sank was loaded with Confederate gold. But if we do find some, we can't tell anybody about it."

"I don't know." Gaff hesitated.

"The water is smoothest where it's deepest," Rhett said calmly.

CHAPTER FIVE

The Sea Monster

"That's why I like you," Rhett said to Gaff.

"Why?" Gaff asked, dragging his crab bucket along beside him.

"Because you're willing to go along on an adventure without getting all worked up over the issue and causing a passel of problems."

"Who said I'm willing to go along on this? It's more dangerous than anything we've ever done."

"True. But think what we can get out of it. Gold. I've never heard the clink of two pieces of gold jiggling together," Rhett said.

"The hot days are about to draw to a close," Gaff said. "Whatever adventure we set our minds to, we have to do it pretty soon."

"You sound like it's boring around here in the wintertime," Rhett countered.

"No. But we go to school then and about the only time we have for crabbing is whatever time is left after the bus drops us off. That's not much."

"I think you've made our decision. If we're going to find a sunken ship and gold, we can't do that late in the afternoon. It takes a good, sunny day, like this one," Rhett claimed.

The boys pulled their boat from the bushes, threw their buckets inside, and started for the oyster banks. Instead of stopping at the crab holes at the oyster banks they oared on until they could see the ocean in the distance. There was nothing quiet about the water today. The wind rustled the cord grass and tiny whitecaps in the inlet swooshed and danced about.

"We've got to find a place where the boat will be protected," Gaff said. "The water's choppier farther on."

"Dad warned me we were in for bad weather today." Rhett dug his oar deep into the water, turning the small boat toward the mudflats. When they had safely steered to the bank, the boys dragged the boat high up on the bank and under the bushes.

"Where do you think a blockade runner would go down?" Gaff asked as they hurried toward the ocean.

"It could be anywhere. It might be in the ocean ahead of us or behind us in the lagoon."

"How are we going to decide where to look?" Gaff asked.

"In about two minutes I'm going to dive in and just go down for a distance and look around," Rhett said.

"Time's passing," Gaff noted. "Why don't we go down right here?"

"I'll go first," Rhett said. "Be back in a jiffy. Then it's your turn." He wandered into deep water, gave a little jump, and dived under.

Though Rhett descended deeper, it remained unexpectedly light around him. He had the sense he was falling but the light boosted his confidence. He could see unidentified shapes moving above him and in front of him. Bits of debris floated about.

Suddenly, the light was hidden by a great shadow. When he looked up, he saw, blocking his path to the surface, a huge mammal. It might be a shark, he thought. If it remained there, how would he escape? How much more time did he have before it would be necessary to breathe deeply? *Not enough.* He wondered about Gaff. What was *he* doing? Could he help if search and rescue became necessary? Would Gaff have the nerve to come into the water? Had he been too hasty in jumping into the briny?

He looked around and saw other shadows, here and there. Shafts of sunlight came in unexpected places. One beam of sun alighted on something, an object Rhett couldn't make out. He stilled his legs and allowed himself to drop further down. Something bright lay on a sort of boulder. He couldn't tell what the boulder was. It could be an animal or a large rock, or even part of a sunken ship, he told himself. The object lying on the boulder was as smooth and bright as the sun on the surface of the sea. As he was trying to figure out what he saw, another great shadow darkened the world he had ventured into. Rhett moved an arm but it wouldn't go where he intended. Something had hold of him. He tried to remove the obstacle with his hand. Whatever the obstruction, it was soft . . . soft and slimy.

Suddenly, Rhett was pulled farther down. The billows surged over him. Seaweed and water grasses wrapped around his head. "Think," he told himself. "There is a way out if you calm down and figure it out." His brain was in a fog. If he had bought a ticket to this dark sea of horrors, he would gladly give it back to get out of his predicament. He began to listen to sounds around him. He knew what he had to do—get to the surface and ashore as quickly as possible. Despite the heavy baggage that had strapped itself to his arm, he used his available hand and feet to propel himself to the surface. Up and up he climbed. The web around his head widened then floated away. The going wasn't as difficult as he had expected. The thing holding onto his arm was helping him to rise. There seemed to be several arms helping him get to the surface. What on earth was this thing? Was it saving his life or trying to do him in? He could feel the pinch as the clutching tentacles squeezed tighter. It could conceivably cut blood circulation. As he got closer to the surface, the wrench on his arm tightened and twisted. Yet another arm seized the back of his neck, and it seemed to be sucking the blood out of his brain. Rhett's face broke the surface and he gulped air into his lungs.

Gaff yelled to him. "Are you all right?"

"Heck, no. Get help. A monster wrench has me in its claws and he's sucking my blood away and squeezing me to death."

Gaff walked a few feet into the water. "Give me your hand."

"I don't have a hand to give. This sea monster has plastered my arms to my body. He has control over my body and I believe my mind too."

Gaff left the water and hurried up the mud banks to look around. Nobody in sight. No boats in Winyah Bay—that was a curiosity.

"Get a rock," Rhett called.

"A what?"

"A rock."

"How big?"

Who cares how big? This monster is killing me and you want to know how big the rock should be. I'll die in a minute if you don't get a rock. Hundreds of suckers are draining my blood."

Gaff found a channeled whelk, about eight inches long. He ran back to where Rhett struggled in the water and waded in. The ocean fed the inlet at that point and waves were breaking all around him. Gaff swam a few feet and held the whelk toward his friend, but Rhett could not reach it.

"What's wrong with you?" Rhett screamed. "Hit this animal and get him away from me."

"Do something and get yourself to shore," Gaff told him.

"Come get me!" Rhett bellowed.

Gaff swam a few feet and tried to stand. He stepped into a drop-off. He went under but quickly surfaced. He held onto the whelk as he swam toward Rhett.

"I'm going to die soon if you don't hit this thing and get him off me," Rhett cried.

Treading water, Gaff struck the creature with the shell and took hold of the soft, slimy wrench that clung to Rhett's back. He pulled with all his might and the creature came loose. "It's an octopus. He's got the biggest head I ever saw. Look at that head!"

"I don't want to see it," Rhett yelled, treading water. "Get it away from me."

The octopus was waving its tentacles about. Then it threw an arm toward Gaff. He knew he had to make an immediate move.

"Listen," Gaff said, "I'm going to swim ashore. Take hold of my foot and I'll drag you."

Rhett held onto Gaff's foot although the other one was splashing in the waves and making suds and foam that enfolded both of them. The boys finally made it to shore where they fell into the pluff mud and lay there, looking at the sky.

"Oh, that feels so good," Rhett said of the soft,

black mud.

"He's gone forever," Gaff said. "We won't see him again."

"Sure hope not."

"What do you mean *hope*? We'll never touch toe to water at this place again," Gaff declared.

"I don't know," Rhett said.

"Are you crazy?"

"No. I'm just being sensible."

"Well that's the least most sensible thing you've ever said. You nearly lost your life to that octopus, and in case you didn't count them, I counted eight of those arms. Only two were holding onto you. What if he had put all eight into action? And that creepy creature is supernatural. He changed color. When he was on your back he was the same color as your skin. When he went into the water he turned blue-green. If you think I'm ever coming back here, you've got another think coming."

"He held on for dear life," Rhett said. "He had the tightest hold I can imagine."

"Those arms have suction cups on them," Gaff explained. "Daddy told me that. They just suck themselves right against your skin and it's nearly impossible to loosen them. They gave a little when I hit him with the whelk. If you come back here and get in that water, then you'll have to bring a new friend. I'm not going into that water again and I cannot imagine why in tarnation you would even think of going back down there."

Rhett hesitated. "I think I will come back and when I do you'll be with me."

"Uh-uh. No way! No way in the world. Get that idea out of your mind."

"I saw something."

"You talk scandalous," Gaff said, opening his eyes wide. "Just forget about this place."

"I saw something."

"I hate this place, and I'll hate you if you insist we come here and go in the water."

"I saw something," Rhett repeated.

"Well what did you see?"

"There's some sort of boulder on the floor of the inlet. Not a large boulder. It could be a rock, a little larger than the whelk you used to get the octopus loose. I saw something lying on that boulder, and it was as bright as the sun on the billows."

"What did you see, Rhett?" Gaff suddenly regretted saying he might ever hate his best friend. He could tell that whatever his friend had seen had affected him greatly.

"Gold."

Gaff's jaw dropped. "You mean real gold?"

"As real as gold can be."

We could be rich, Gaff thought. "How're we going to get some of it?"

"We'll figure out a way," Rhett promised.

"Even considering the octopus?" Gaff asked.

"Even considering the octopus."

Before heading home, Rhett and Gaff sat awhile and looked out at the inlet they enjoyed so much. They considered the enormous estate, The Barony, on one side and North Island in the distance. This place was important to the people of South Carolina. Several species of crabs, clams, and myriads of fish were here for the taking. The Barony was privately owned, so there were no prowlers or people with intent to desecrate the land—except for the poachers, and Gaff's dad took care of them. It was also a place of danger, as Rhett's father had pointed out many times. Rhett had thought about that when he discovered the octopus tentacles still attached to his right arm. He tore them loose and threw them away.

"That octopus left a red trail behind him when he swam away," Gaff said.

"I don't care if he left a rainbow of colors. I'm glad I didn't see it," Rhett answered.

"Hush. I hear something," Gaff said.

"What?"

"That tell-tale sound. You know what I mean?"

"Don't have a clue," Rhett said.

"The sound of mullet. A whole school of them."

"We should've known the mullet are running. The seagulls are rising and dipping, a sure sign."

Gaff watched the rise and fall of the seagulls—soaring nearly out of sight into the sky and dropping quickly to the water. "And if we want more than mullet, we know where the red snapper and bass are. We'll have to come back tomorrow and bring the seine."

"There's some kind of special providence that gives gulls their ability to fly nearly to the sky and drop in an instant to the water—that's what Dad says," Rhett offered. "And there's something special about the mullet and the way they run in schools and know where to go." He looked at Gaff. "I wish there were something special about me. We didn't get any crab claws today. We'll have to do something special tomorrow. The only thing is, the inlet is forty feet wide and our gill-seine net is only thirty feet."

"We'll have to spank the water," Gaff offered. "After you stretch the net and we get it grounded, you grab an oar and whack that water like it did something you told it not to do. That school of mullet will move right into the net. We'll get a barrel of mullet. Tomorrow."

"What if an atomic bomb falls on The Barony tonight?" Rhett asked.

"Don't be so creepy. No atomic bomb will fall on us. General Marshall will see to that."

"This is a good place," Rhett said thoughtfully, even as he remembered the close call with the octopus. When the octopus had him by the arm and neck, he believed he would never set foot at this place again. He stood, conjuring up images of the history of the area, where the inlet and the sea shook hands, as he and Gaff liked to say.

"Dad said years ago a canal was formed to bring sea water into the rice fields. This inlet was one of those canals, and the marshes are abandoned rice fields. There's usually good fishing where the canal meets the ocean."

"Don't forget the hunting," Gaff reminded. "Birds, geese, turkeys, and ducks flock to these old rice fields and fatten up for Thanksgiving day."

"That time's a-coming," Rhett said. "For now, we'll settle for mullet." He looked around. "We'll need a boat to carry the fish"

"Yeah. Let's just keep it close. We'll need it to hold our other stuff too."

CHAPTER SIX

Spanking the Water

Next morning, Gaff and Rhett sat in their ten-foot cypress bateau, awaiting the tell-tale sign of mullet. Suddenly they heard the thudding of the water coming from the ocean into the canal.

"They're here! The mullet are here!" Rhett yelled.

He and Gaff pulled furiously to drag their boat out of the water. Standing on shore, they watched the fish swim into the creek.

"There're millions of them," Gaff called out.

"Zillions," Rhett answered.

When the fish had all entered the creek, Rhett and Gaff gently pushed their boat back into the water and oared to the far side of the inlet. They positioned the pole attached to the gill-seine net. They hurried back to the other shore and staked the opposite end of the net. The race was on. Although the net did not stretch fully from one side of the inlet to the other, it would snare a good catch.

The boys left their boat close to the net and they took their oars and walked along the shore until they found a place they believed was good for spanking the water.

"Give her a whack!" Rhett yelled.

Gaff's oar beat the water like it was engaged in battle. Rhett did the same, using his oar to hammer the water as though it were a giant serpent. The frightened mullet made a quick aboutface toward the sea.

At the sound of the mullet jumping, Rhett and Gaff threw the oars down and ran for the net. Thousands of mullet were caught in the holes of the net or huddled against them. As the boys went into the water to begin pulling the fish away from the net, they realized that dozens were burying themselves in the mud under the net. Others were jumping over it.

Suddenly the fish stopped jumping. Rhett knew that meant something in the water frightened them. As he held up the seine, he felt a big wave rise to his shoulder. Moving slowly in front of him, he saw the fin of a great shark pass along the downstream side of the net. It had come in with the tide and was prowling for dinner.

Rhett tried to move toward the boat, hollering for Gaff to follow him, but he realized he was stuck fast in the mud.

Gaff stopped spanking the water. He wanted to get to the seine, where he thought his friend was having fun taking out the mullet. Rhett could hear his friend tramping along through the mud. He shouted for Gaff to come free him, but his voice was lost in the wind and lapping of the water. He was alone there in the mud without any weapon, and the water was up to his neck.

The shark had now reached the end of the seine. For a while the creature seemed confused, then it turned toward Rhett. Rhett beat the water with his hands, screamed at the shark, and cried wildly for Gaff. The shark swam steadily on. It was now only ten feet away. No chance of escape. Rhett thought quickly, then catching the seine, he lifted it violently as high as he could, ducked under it while pulling his feet out of the mud. He came up on the other

side and dropped the net back in place. The net was his only defense against the cold-blooded monster, but that was enough. For a moment, though, those terrible jaws were way too close.

The shark rushed by. He swam a distance, then turned and headed for the seine. Just before he reached the net, he swerved.

Suddenly, Rhett could hear Gaff shouting, "Shark! Shark! Help me or he'll get me." The great gray creature raced toward Gaff. It was bearing down on its prey when Rhett's strong hands gripped his friend's arms and pulled him away. The boys raced for shore. They climbed into their waiting boat, where they sat, catching their breath.

"We'd better think of a way to get that seine out of the water and fill this boat with mullet," Rhett said. "The shark has found another feeding place."

"Let's go." Gaff jumped out of the boat

Rhett and Gaff pushed and pulled the boat as near the seine net as possible. They tugged at the net, but it wouldn't move. "It's loaded down with mullet," Gaff said. "We're never going to get the net out of the water while it's filled with fish."

"Think of something," Rhett growled.

Gaff walked along the shore but saw no sign of the shark. "Push the boat over here," he called.

Rhett pushed the boat toward his friend.

"You go first," Rhett said. "I still have scars from the octopus."

Gaff walked gingerly, taking baby steps. He leaned over and pulled two mullet out. As he pulled the fish out, Rhett put them in the boat.

"If you see that shark again, let me know," Gaff called over a shoulder.

"He's nowhere to be seen," Rhett said. "Keep the mullet coming. I'm stacking them up."

They worked together quietly, with Gaff freeing the fish and Rhett stacking them in the boat, listening for approaching sea monsters. Before an hour had passed, the boat was almost too full to accommodate the boys. They pulled in the net and poles and hid them in the bushes to pick up on their next journey to the inlet.

The trip home wasn't the easiest thing in the world. Rhett and Gaff oared for a few seconds then fought the fish with their oars. When they reached the spot where they would dock the boat, they had lost about a third of their catch.

"I know where there's a sack," Gaff said.

"Get it," Rhett urged.

Rhett kept the fish in place as best he could until Gaff returned with the sack. A few fish wouldn't fit but one tow sack full of mullet was a good catch.

Rhett's mother, Alice, was working on her knees in her flower garden when the boys arrived with the mullet. Mrs. Gingyard stood and looked at the fish. She told Rhett to keep about a dozen and take the others to Gaff's home.

As the boys turned to walk away, Mrs. Gingyard noticed a red blotch on Rhett's neck. "What caused that redness?" she asked.

"It's no picnic to catch mullet," he explained. "The fish were jumping every which way." He was careful not to mention the shark or the octopus.

Mrs. Gingyard gave her son a quick hug and cautioned him to be careful.

"Bye, Mom."

"We'll have mullet for supper," she said.

CHAPTER SEVEN

The Tree That Caught a Fish

"Know what I wish we were having for supper?" Alice Gingyard was a terrific homemaker and spent a lot of time thinking about her family's meals. This particular night the Gingyards sat together on the porch, enjoying the nocturnal sounds of The Barony.

"No, Mom. What would you like?" Rhett asked.

"A big bass. We've had mullet until it's coming out my ears. I haven't had a good bass in months."

Mr. Gingyard looked across the porch at his only child. "Son, Mom does so much for us. She keeps our house clean and our clothes in order and food on the table and she rarely asks for anything. What if I get my duck boat and we go bass fishing tomorrow?"

"Will you go with us, Mom?" Rhett asked.

"You betcha."

"Can Gaff go too?" Rhett asked.

"Of course," Mr. Gingyard responded. "It wouldn't be an outing without Gaff."

The next morning the Gingyards and Gaff made their way to the dock where the duck boat was waiting. Mr. Gingyard helped his wife and the boys into the boat. Fishing poles made from canes from the bamboo thicket near the marshes lay in the bottom, near the vessel's stern. Rhett's dad had his favorite rod and reel and fishing lures. His mom had made bait from her own recipe. It looked like a ball of biscuit dough.

Unlike the cypress dugout canoe Rhett and Gaff used for their adventures, Mr. Gingyard's duck boat had a small motor. He started it up and they were off.

On the way to the Wiley Wreck and the sight of a wrecked schooner, not far offshore, where he believed with all his heart that bass were waiting to take a hook, Mr. Gingyard shared his knowledge of olden times in the area. "In some of the old, abandoned rice fields of the Lowcountry," Mr. Gingyard began, "there are still canals and little ditches. Some of these are good fishing grounds for big mouth bass. The people who lived on the plantations during the rice-producing days—as well as their descendants today—called the fish trout. We use our duck boats for fishing in the canals today. Long ago, the guide sat in the stern. Sometimes such a boat would glide through a narrow ditch under the overhanging trees, draped with Spanish moss. Along the edges of the ditches, there was a thick growth of bushes and briars."

"Oh, Lucas, I see such a place," Alice Gingyard said. May we fish there?"

"Over there, under the oak trees?"

"Oh, yes. Let's stop there. It's so lovely."

"But the tree limbs are draped in Spanish moss."

"That's why it's so lovely."

Mr. Gingyard turned the boat toward the trees and found a place to tie up. He baited hooks for Rhett, Gaff, and his wife, then worked on his own lure.

Mrs. Gingyard settled back and took a deep breath of the salty air. "The Lowcountry is lovelier here in the old canals than anywhere else."

"Tell us a story, Dad," Rhett prompted.

"See that brick tower in the distance, far to the south?" Mr. Gingyard responded, as he continued to work on his lure.

"Yes, sir. What is it?"

"That was built as a place a refuge during hurricanes. We still have vicious hurricanes in the South Carolina Low Country but, long ago, most houses were not as substantially built. When a wind arose—and especially if someone had recently noticed a ring around the moon—the people who worked on the large estates believed a deadly storm was about to crash on shore. They lived in small cabins, and that brick tower was where they waited out the storm."

"What about the ring around the moon?" Gaff asked.

Mr. Gingyard gave his fishing line a jerk to tighten it. He cast it into deep water and reeled in a few feet of line. "There were no national weather reporting systems during that day and time. The people had no way of predicting what the weather was going to do, except for omens or signs. They believed a ring around the moon meant bad weather."

"I've been through several hurricanes," Mrs. Gingyard said. "And there were times during those storms when I wished I were in that brick tower."

"It's perfectly safe. I don't think any storm would be powerful enough to blow it down," Mr. Gingyard said.

"Are there a lot of those brick towers in the Low Country?" Rhett asked.

"That's the only one I know of."

"Who does it belong it?" Gaff asked.

"Mr. Blackhall. Although I don't recall it ever being used during a hurricane. The people who worked the rice fields are gone now, and Mr. Blackhall uses the estate for hunting. His Washington friends just love to come here and hunt ducks, deer, wild turkeys, you name it. But we have better-built houses now."

"Are we safe?" Rhett asked.

His father nodded. "About the worst we get is a

power outage and trees down. We have a lot of work to do here after a hurricane, but as far as I know, no lives have been lost in recent years.

"Oh, mercy! Mercy! Help me!" Alice Gingyard shouted, her fishing pole bent into an arc. Something very heavy pulled on the end of her line.

Mr. Gingyard threw his rod and reel to the bottom of the boat and stepped over Gaff to get to his wife.

Just then, Mrs. Gingyard screamed and let go of the fishing pole. It flew out of her hands and high into the air.

"Oh, my. I lost my big fish," she moaned.

Mr. Gingyard grabbed an oar and eased the boat to the shore. Tree limbs and Spanish moss hung just overhead. Mrs. Gingyard stood to climb ashore.

"Don't leave the boat," her husband shouted. "There are snakes here. Water moccasins."

She eased back to her seat.

"If you ever look down the white cottony throat of a water moccasin and see the big sharp teeth, you'll never forget it. Stay where you are," Mr. Gingyard cautioned.

"I'll find the fish," Rhett said.

"Rhett, you stay put," his father warned.

Mr. Gingyard got hold of a piece of his wife's fishing line and began to pull. There was no resistance. "Nothing is on this line," he said. "Alice, are you sure you had a fish on the hook?"

"I'm sure. Absolutely sure. Don't make fun of me."

"No one is making fun of you, honey, but, as you can see, nothing is on this line."

Mrs. Gingyard stood, holding onto the shoulders of her son. She held the line and eyed it from one end to the other. "The fishing pole is gone."

Rhett leaned over the side of the boat and looked around. "No fish here, Mom. You let the big one get away."

Mrs. Gingyard eased herself back to her seat. "It's just like me to hook a huge fish and no one knows about it but me. He took the pole with him."

"Mom," Rhett soothed, "you probably hooked a tree root, or an old shoe, or something like that. It fell off before you landed it." He continued to look in the water.

"Mrs. Gingyard, think back," Gaff said. "You had something heavy on the line. When did you feel the line go limp?"

Mrs. Gingyard thought for a moment. It was heavy until it was way over my head. When it went limp, the fish and the pole were gone. Just like that." She snapped her fingers.

"I'm going to find the pole," Gaff said. He focused his eyes on the foliage, vines, and roots, searching hard for any sign. "I see it!"

"Where?" Mr. Gingyard asked.

"It's there, under that tree limb. A few inches

are sticking up."

"I see it," Rhett said. "Now if only we can find the fish."

"You won't find the fish," Mr. Gingyard said.

"Why?" Rhett asked.

"Because he's back in the inlet and headed to sea."

"I'm ready to go home," Mrs. Ginyard complained.

"I don't think the fish are biting today," Mr. Gingyard said, reeling in his line.

Everybody was preparing their lines for the trip home when Alice Gingyard said, "Something is moving in the Spanish moss."

"What Spanish moss?" Rhett asked.

"That big clump right over my head," Mrs. Gingyard answered.

"I don't see anything," Rhett said. "Must be the breeze."

"It's moving all right," she responded, "but it's because of my fish."

Gaff stood and looked carefully. "Something really *is* in that clump of Spanish moss."

"It can't be," Rhett said. He removed a pocket knife from a hip pocket and reached up to the mass, pulling a hunk away from the large cluster of moss. Something heavy fell into his mother's lap. She jumped up, screaming. "Oh! Oh! My fish! It's my fish!"

It was true. The large bass had come loose from the fishing pole and become lodged in the thick Spanish moss.

Mr. Gingyard took hold of the fish, put a finger in its mouth and held on until he could run a cord through the mouth and out of the gill to tie the fish to the boat. Its tail swished this way and that until it was secured.

"My wife's catch," he said. "She and the Spanish moss landed a whopper. I'll clean the fish and Alice will no doubt serve it for breakfast tomorrow morning. Gaff, you're invited."

CHAPTER EIGHT

The Alligator

Gaff stopped mid-step. "Look. Alligator."

"Let him be," Rhett said, carefully putting down his bucket. "He'll pass and we'll get our crabs."

"Funny," Gaff said.

"What's funny about an alligator? They're dangerous, not funny."

"It's funny the way they walk," Gaff answered. "They have those funny little short, stubby legs that lift them off the ground."

Rhett gazed at the animal. "We mostly see them lying in the sun on the grassy bank or swimming in the inlet. It's not often we see one actually walking from one place to another. But that armor-plated demon is making a move. Be still. We don't want him to see us."

"Where do you think he's going?" Gaff whispered.

"Who knows? He's not headed toward the ocean. Maybe he's going to the marshes. Or maybe he—or she—has a nest somewhere. Dad says the female 'gators talk to their babies while the little ones are in the egg."

"Now, how in the world would your dad know that? Do they sing lullabies to the babies?"

"Dad says in years past the marine biology department of the university sent a professor here to determine whether the female alligator communicates with her babies while they're in the eggs. The professor determined the mama 'gator does communicate with her young while they're still in the egg." Rhett said.

"Oh, come on!" Gaff laughed.

"No, really. The mama grunts, and then a faint little grunt comes from the egg. That's common knowledge. And when the babies climb out of the egg and the nest, they crawl straight to their mama."

Gaff shook his head. "I've never heard of such a thing."

The boys watched the alligator until it crawled a safe distance away.

"Say, Gaff, you'd be a good scientist. What do you plan to do when you grow up and leave The Barony?"

"I don't know. . . . To tell you the truth, I don't ever want to leave The Barony. Do you?"

"No, but Dad says I'll go to college," Rhett answered.

"Which one?"

"Maybe the University in Columbia, where he went, or The Citadel in Charleston, where your dad went. Mama likes Wofford in Spartanburg—that's upstate, where her family lives."

"I'll go off to college first," Gaff said, "and I hope you'll go where I go. Best friends, you know."

"Oh, look!" Rhett's attention was caught by movement in the distance. "There's Mr. and Mrs. Cribb, of Clam Cove. I wonder what they're doing over here. They don't usually go crabbing in this area."

"I believe that's the first time I've ever seen Mr. Cribb when he's not on the tractor, cutting grass or clearing a garden."

"Dad said he's a hard worker and she goes at it the very same. He says Mrs. Cribb works as hard as any man he's ever known."

"What does she do?"

"She can roof a house," Rhett answered, "or repair any farm machine or cut a field of hay and haul it in and bale it."

"Do they have any kids?"

"Nope. Just the two of them. Dad says she worries about what's going to happen to them when they die. Mr. Blackhall found out about that and he promised them he would see to it they get a decent funeral and burial. She was real happy about that."

"Oh, no. No! No!" Gaff yelled. "Mr. Cribb is kicking the 'gator. He's going to have that funeral before he expected it."

Rhett took off running toward the Cribbs and calling out, "Don't do that! Stop kicking the alligator or he'll bite you!"

Gaff, whose legs were longer than Rhett's, overtook his friend and flew toward the couple. "Stop, Mr. Cribb. Don't kick it."

"He's trying to bite me," Mr. Cribb said between gasps. "He's trying to kill me." Just then, the alligator groaned and let out a bellow.

Mrs. Cribb walked up with a large stick in her hand and looked on as the alligator swallowed Mr. Cribb's leg.

"The alligator's swallowed his whole leg, up to the hip joint!" Rhett yelled.

"All foot and shoe down in the 'gator's belly," Mrs. Cribb moaned.

Mr. Cribb was writhing in pain and flailing his arms. His wife was hitting the alligator on the back with the stick, but the animal didn't budge.

Mrs. Cribb stood back. "I'm studying what to do," she screeched. After a few seconds she threw a leg over the alligator and sat down on its back. Leaning forward, she worked a hand into its mouth and on down its throat until she came to a pocket in her husband's trousers. "I'm after that old hawk-bill knife he always carries," she yelled, pulling the knife out. She leaned over the alligator's head and raked the blade of the knife across the alligator's throat. She stood and, with the help of Gaff and Rhett, pulled her husband's leg from the stomach of the scaly beast.

Mr. Cribb leaned on his wife's shoulder. "It's mighty like Jonah in the whale 'cept the 'gator didn't take all of me into its belly," he groaned.

Mrs. Cribb held tight to her husband as they started home.

Rhett and Gaff stared at each other.

"Your dad's right about them being strong," Gaff said.

The boys watched the couple until they were out of sight.

"You still want to go crabbing?" Rhett asked.

"Sure. We need crabmeat at our house," Gaff answered.

"Well, let's go then," Rhett agreed, "and hope we don't see another alligator walking across the road."

CHAPTER NINE

Copperhead!

"Let's go somewhere different today." It was a bright sunny afternoon and Rhett was ready for a new adventure. "Does your mama need any stone crabs for the Blackhalls' supper?"

"No," Gaff answered. "She's cooking quail pie, made from birds left over from dinner."

"Umm!" Rhett's mouth began to water for a good helping of hot quail pie with peas and rice.

"What's on your mind?' Gaff asked.

"I thought I'd ask Dad if we could drive Mr. Blackhall's old Chevy. We could go over to the estuary and see what's jumping."

"Your dad's not very generous with that old car," Gaff said.

"We won't take any chances. But if we did slide into a ditch, do you think they would arrest us? My dad and yours are the only law enforcement people at The Barony."

"We wouldn't be arrested but if we wreck that car they might do something that would make us wish we were in jail," Gaff declared.

"I'll tell Dad we'll be careful. We won't go anywhere except Clam Cove and Danseuse Drifts and the estuary. If he gets worried, he'll jump in the pickup and come find us."

"If you've got the nerve, go on then. I'm up for it."

Mr. Gingyard held the keys up and shook them. "This is not our car, Rhett, and you know that. If you take any chances and slide into a ditch or mire down in the swamp, I'll have to answer for it."

"I'll be careful, Dad. Promise."

Rhett, Gaff, and Mr. Gingyard left for the garage where the Blackhall vehicles were parked. Bamboo fishing poles were propped against the side of the building.

"I'll drop a couple of these fishing canes in the trunk just in case you boys want to try your hand at hooking a fish," Mr. Gingyard said.

"Thanks, Dad."

"Thanks, Mr. Gingyard," Gaff added.

Mr. Gingyard watched the boys until the Chevy was out of sight. He felt uneasy when others used one of the Blackhall vehicles. There were a lot of ways to get into trouble at The Barony. One had to remain aware of conditions and stay alert.

Rhett drove around the barn and on toward Clam Cove. It was unusual to see no people about. Leaving Clam Cove and heading toward Danseuse Drifts and the ocean, Rhett suddenly pulled the car over to the side of the sandy lane.

"Why are you stopping?" Gaff asked.

"Look! See that tiny face on the ground between the wax myrtle bushes? It's just barely showing among the leaves."

"I don't see it. What is it?" Gaff asked.

"A pit viper. There's a pit on each side of its head, between the eye and the nostril."

"Is it a rattler?"

"No. There're plenty of cane brake rattlers around, but this one's a copperhead, sure as my name's Rhett."

"I see it! It's a copperhead all right."

"He's moving. Going into its coil, ready to strike. If he were a rattler, he'd be sounding his bells by now," Rhett said.

"Look at the skin," Gaff pointed out. "Light brown with darker scrolls that look like an hour glass, big on the ends and wasp-waist thin in the middle."

"That's a copperhead," Rhett said. "And don't let that forked tongue put you in a trance. That thing's full of venom."

"Why did you stop?" Gaff asked.

"I'm letting that monster get on his way. I'll wait him out."

"He's not going anywhere," Gaff said. "He's in his coil and ready to strike."

"I'll move on slowly and outsmart him," Rhett said.

Rhett gave the gas pedal a little prod and the Chevy moved ahead by inches. "Where is it?" Rhett asked. "I can't see him. Where'd he go? Did I run over it? Is it dead?"

"It's not where it was. It moved," Gaff said. "And you stopped right at it. It might be on the tire or under the hood somewhere."

Rhett advanced the car a couple feet. "Can you see it?"

Gaff looked back. He opened the door and hung out to see what he could see. "It's nowhere in the road and it's not where it was when we first saw it. I think it's attached to the car. He leaned out further.

"Close the door. We're getting away from here," Rhett said, moving the car a few inches.

At that moment, Gaff's hand slipped from the

door handle and he flipped out of the car, head-first.

Rhett brought the car to a stop, got out and ran to Gaff, who was crying.

"It bit me. I felt the punctures from my knee to my ankle. It was the snake, I'm sure of it."

Rhett helped Gaff up and into the front seat of the car. He flew to the trunk of the Chevy and took a fishing cane. "I'm going to kill that devil," he said. "Do you know where the snake is, Gaff?"

Before Gaff could answer, the snake, again in its coil, its neck extended and its forked tongue darting in and out, was on the edge of the road. Rhett beat him mercilessly with the fishing pole. He wasn't sure he had killed the serpent, but he jumped into the car, turned around in the road, and started for home.

"What are we going to do?" Gaff asked.

"Don't know yet. Are you feeling any pain?"

"None," Gaff answered.

"Can you see any punctures in your leg?" Rhett asked.

Gaff was wearing short pants and his eyes took in far more punctures than he wanted to see. "There must be hundreds. Each tiny hole has a bit of blood, just a little bit, not even half a drop."

When they reached home, Rhett saw his dad in the yard and yelled for him to come quickly. "Gaff's been bitten by a snake, a copperhead."

"How do you know?" Mr. Gingyard asked.

"Look at his leg."

Mr. Gingyard told Rhett and Gaff to get in the pickup. He jumped into the truck and the tires scratched the sand as the vehicle lurched forward. "We've got to get to Dr. Taylor, and soon," Mr. Gingyard said. "How did this happen?"

"The snake was on the side of the road but then disappeared. We looked around, every which way, but there was no sign of him. I moved the Chevy ahead, very slowly. Gaff opened the door and leaned out to see if the snake was attached to the car. As he lowered his head and looked at the lower part of the car, he lost his balance and fell out, head-first. By the time I stopped the car and got out, Gaff had been bitten a hundred times."

"Maybe not a hundred times, but we've got to get to Dr. Taylor," Mr. Gingyard said. "He can treat Gaff with anti-venom. . . . I just thought of something." Mr. Gingyard wheeled the pickup in a U turn. "We've got to take the snake with us. Dr. Taylor will have to see it to make a decision about the medication."

Rhett and Gaff said nothing but sat wide-eyed in the truck as Mr. Gingyard pulled the truck up to the garage, ran in and came back with a large jar. "You think the snake is still where you left it?"

"I gave him a pretty good beating," Rhett said. "He should be in the road after we pass Clam Cove."

The snake was lying where Rhett and Gaff had

left it. Mr. Gingyard took a few steps into the woods and picked up a tree limb that had blown from a tree. He gave the serpent a few whacks that were sure to finish him off, then raked him into the jar and they were off to the doctor's office.

The nurse placed Gaff on a stretcher and rolled him into another room, leaving Rhett and his father in the waiting area.

Dr. Taylor leaned over the leg. "How many punctures are there?" he asked Gaff.

"There must be a hundred," Gaff said.

"I'm going to operate on the snake. Wait here," Dr. Taylor said. "I have to know if it expelled all its venom into your leg."

"Where else would it go?" Gaff asked.

"There's a possibility the snake has bitten a rat within the past twenty-four hours. If not and he passed all the venom to your leg, you'll be given anti-venom medication."

While Dr. Taylor was out of the room he also made a call to Duke University's poison control center and consulted with doctors there.

"Well, young man," Dr. Taylor said, when he walked back into the examining room, "your leg was the recipient of all of the snake's venom. We're going to administer the maximum dosage of horse serum."

Quickly and efficiently, the nurse and doctor washed Gaff's leg. The nurse held a hand at Gaff's cheek to soothe him while the doctor injected the leg with the horse serum. Within an hour, Gaff's leg had puffed until it did not resemble a leg. There was no indention where the ankle should have been and there appeared to be no toes. The swelling flesh was frightening.

"Can I have something for pain?" Gaff asked.

"No," the doctor answered. "Pain medication goes to the heart. A snake's venom also goes to the heart. I'm afraid your heart cannot accommodate both applications."

The nurse went out and came back with a pan of crushed ice and placed it on the huge mass that had once been a leg. Gaff was made as comfortable as possible.

"Why did this happen to me?" Gaff whined, tears in his eyes.

"Because you are a boy," the doctor answered. "You'd be surprised how many snake bites I treat each year. You must consider that you live at The Barony, a place known for its wildlife, including snakes. Especially snakes."

A call was made to Gaff's parents and they arrived shortly at the doctor's office.

The nurse and doctor remained with Gaff all night, and Rhett and his dad and Gaff's parents sat in an outer room. The next day Gaff was allowed to go home and instructed to lie in bed for three weeks, keeping his leg elevated on a stack of pillows.

Rhett visited Gaff each day and they talked about their adventures at The Barony. Despite all its natural risks, they agreed they wouldn't want to live anywhere else. Gaff promised to watch his step and never get close to a snake again.

Gaff was growing restless cooped up in bed and itched for a new adventure. Rhett visited every day and they talked of things they'd do once Gaff was back to normal.

"This snakebite has been about as bad as the atomic bomb," Gaff whined.

"No. It wasn't that bad," Rhett said. "When the bomb hits, everything will be burned up."

The boys talked at some length about General Marshall. Gaff felt proud that he knew the only person in charge of the bomb. It was General Marshall who would decide if and when it would be used. Rhett speculated that the general must be the smartest man in the whole world for the president to bestow so much responsibility on him.

"Is General Marshall coming back to The Barony?" Rhett asked Gaff's mother.

"Oh, mercy, yes," she said. "You couldn't keep him away when the ducks and Canadian geese arrive. He'll be right here."

"Will Mr. Blackhall ask him about the bomb?" Gaff wanted to know.

"You can bet on it. And I will be sure that you

and Rhett are within hearing distance. I think it's important you boys know something of General Marshall and hear what he has to say about the bomb."

"Good!" Rhett said. "I want to know about that bomb."

"You must understand, Rhett, that even though the swelling is going down in Gaffney's leg, he has not fully recovered. That will take weeks."

Rhett looked at Gaff. "What'll we do for fun?"

"Both of your dads have talked about that," Mrs. Dorn said. "They're going to take you on frequent long jaunts in the truck, and you'll identify animals, trees, birds, and many things at The Barony that you haven't paid much attention to."

"I'm ready to go," Gaff said.

"Not right away. Dr. Taylor will decide just when you can be up and about," Mrs. Dorn said.

Three weeks from the day of that conversation, Gaff and Rhett were begging for their first excursion of The Barony.

CHAPTER TEN

Daffy Deer

"Gaffney, do you feel like taking a ride in the car?" Mr. Dorn asked. "It's Thursday, and my duties always seem lighter on Thursdays."

"Yes, sir!" Gaff answered. "Where're we going?"

"We'll just slowly make our way around The Barony. I'll take a look at things as we ride around. We can stop and see if Rhett wants to go."

Rhett climbed in fast when they reached his house. "Jeepers creepers, I'm so glad to see Gaff up and around, I'll go anywhere." Rhett sat on the front seat and left the backseat open so Gaff could stretch out his leg and get comfortable.

"Where're we going?" Rhett asked.

"There's such a network of roads here we can go almost anywhere, but I thought we'd drive by Clam Cove," Mr. Dorn said.

"Abraham's wife died a while back," Rhett said.

"Yes. I came over to the little Mount Moriah Church for the funeral," Mr. Dorn responded. "Her death was a loss to the Clam Cove community. She was a good woman and helped a lot of people."

"Hey, look," Gaff spoke up. "There's a wild boar."

"We'll pass him by," Mr. Dorn said. "He's digging for roots. Don't miss the tusks, near the mouth. Do you boys see that?"

"Uh-huh," Gaff said, his nose pressed against the window glass.

"Those tusks can tear up a man, much less a boy," Mr. Dorn explained. "If you see a wild boar, get away as fast as you can."

Three more wild boars were spotted before the car made the last turn at Clam Cove. Abraham was sitting on his porch. "Let's stop for a chat," Mr. Dorn said. "Gaffney, are you up to it?"

"Yes, sir. I'm just glad to be outside."

"Get outa that car and come on in," Abraham called.

Rhett, Gaff, and Mr. Dorn sat on the porch steps. Abraham continued sitting in an old half-broken ladder-back chair near the porch rail. He looked at Rhett. "So. Your name's *Rhett.*"

"Yes, sir. That's me," the boy answered.

"I know the Rhetts—know all about 'em."

"Well, I believe Rhett here's mother was a Rhett, from Beaufort," Mr. Dorn said.

"That was at a later time," Abraham said. "The Rhetts I knew were way back yonder."

"Tell us about them," Rhett invited.

Abraham slapped a knee. "I'm going way back now. Way back. My mammy and her daddy and mammy belonged to the Rhett family when my mammy was a little girl. She recalled a lot of things after she joined the Rhetts. She lived with them until she was just turning twelve years old, then she went to Columbia to work for John T. Rhett."

"Do you know anything about this, Rhett?" Mr. Dorn asked.

"I've heard talk about the branches of my mother's family that lived in Charleston and Beaufort, and Columbia," Rhett answered.

"My mammy never worked in the field at Beaufort, nor after she came to Columbia," Abraham went on. "She was kept on duty in the big house and learned to sew and make garments, quilts, and things. She learned to read, write, and cipher, and she could sing many of the church songs of them days. She played with the white Rhett chillun, and she tell me 'bout them things.

"She tell us chillun that the Rhetts sho' was the 'big folks' of South Carolina and I reckons that is so. I know right where John T. Rhett lived in Columbia. He lived at the house now number 1420 Washington Street, right 'cross the street from where the parsonage of the Washington Street Methodist Church now stands. I go there with Mammy and played 'round the yard. Mammy worked there as long as she was able to serve a-tall. She take sick and die in 1883. John T. Rhett was mayor of the city three times, in 1882, 1884, and in 1886.

"And I knew R. Goodwin Rhett of Charleston. I

sho' knows him. He was born in Columbia but moved to Charleston many years ago and, like the brilliant man he was, he climbed to the top as the mayor of Charleston, a big banker, and president of the Chamber of Commerce of the United States. So you see, my mammy was lucky in living with such a fine family. She say the Rhetts been the finest in the state since the time when Colonel William Rhett go out in his battleships to chase and kill pirates, in the days when Carolina was ruled by the King of England. She say the Rhetts own many big estates in Beaufort County and raise big crops of rice and sea island cotton. She say the sea island cotton was so costly it was handpicked by people and placed in hundred pound sacks. Then it was shipped to France and the growers reap a rich harvest. The Rhetts have them good old books, swords, guns, windlasses, and things like that, in a room at the John T. Rhett home. And it all start with Colonel William Rhett back in the Carolina colony days."

"He's my ancestor," Rhett said. "Colonel William Rhett was appointed by Governor Johnson to hunt down Stede Bonnet and other pirates and they were hanged in the Charleston harbor. My mother can tell you all about that. She named me for Colonel William Rhett."

"Well, I think it's about time we were moving on," Mr. Dorn said as he rose. Abraham invited them to come back any time and hear more of his stories.

Back in the car, they headed toward Danseuse Drifts, on the far side of a wooded area.

"Look," Gaff said. "A toy. No, it's not a toy, it's a stuffed animal."

"It looks just like a stuffed dog I have," Rhett said.

Mr. Dorn pulled the car to the side of the road. "That's a newborn deer," he said. "The mother's gone, but she took the time to clean him up before she left."

"Did she abandon her baby?" Gaff asked.

"It's not uncommon for a mother deer to abandon a baby," Mr. Dorn said. "You remember the wild boar we saw a little while ago? If they find this little deer it'll be their dinner tonight."

"Oh, Dad!" Gaff said. "I'm getting out. I want to see the baby deer."

Before Gaff reached the deer, his father and Rhett were with him. The tiny deer made an effort to rise but fell back. Lying in the underbrush of the trees, the deer looked small and helpless.

The little animal tried again to get up. He rose on all four legs, but they were wobbly and he fell back into the grasses.

Gaff reached for him.

"Don't touch him," Mr. Dorn cautioned. "His mother might be watching us. She could attack you and you're not quite up to it, having been attacked by a copperhead."

Oblivious to any danger, Gaff picked up the deer. It cuddled close to his cheek. "I'm taking him home," he said.

Rhett stood aside, watching and listening to the exchange between Gaff and his father.

"Do you have any idea what raising a tiny deer involves?" Mr. Dorn asked.

"Feeding, washing, talking to him. Dad, he needs me. Don't say no. He'll be company for me while my leg gets well. I need *him*, Dad."

"What do you feed him?" Rhett asked.

"We'll give him some milk and pretty soon he'll be eating and grazing," Mr. Dorn said, acknowledging his approval to take the deer home.

"Thanks, Dad. Thank you a million times."

"What are you going to name him?" Rhett asked.

"I don't like Toy, but that came to mind when we saw him. What about Daffy Deer? We found him where the daffodils grow."

"You could find worse names," Mr. Dorn said.

Gaff nuzzled the baby deer to his cheek and said, "Daffy Deer, you've got a new home."

"If we don't take him," Mr. Dorn said, "the wild boars will get him and maybe his mother as well."

"He'll be safe with us." Gaff beamed with pride as he carried his new friend to the truck.

CHAPTER ELEVEN

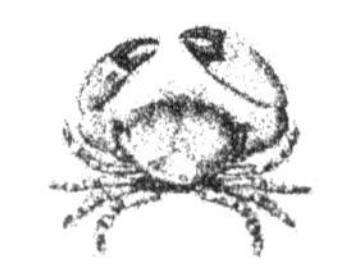

The Claw

"Dad, Rhett and I need to get some crab claws." Gaff strode into the living room, with Rhett and Daffy Deer following close on his heels.

Mr. Dorn put down his newspaper and pushed his reading glasses to his forehead. "Son, I wish I could let you go but I'm not sure your leg has properly healed for such an outing. There's a lot of walking in the marsh and rowing the boat in the inlet, not to mention getting the crab out of the deep hole. Think you're up to it?"

"I'm going to do most of the work," Rhett offered. "I promise you, Mr. Dorn, Gaff won't put his hand near a crab hole."

"Please, Dad. PUHLEEZE. And can Daffy Deer go too?"

"Absolutely not. Daffy Deer would be a distraction. You need no distractions when you do something so dangerous as digging for stone crabs."

"But *I* can go? C'mon, Rhett. They need some crab meat at the big house. I heard Mama say so."

"I don't have my bucket," Rhett said.

"You can carry mine," Gaff said as he leaned

down and kissed Daffy Deer on the top of the head. It was clear the boy and the little deer—which, indeed, looked like a stuffed toy animal—had bonded.

Rhett carried the bucket as they walked through the marsh. Gaff's leg was still a bit puffy, but the swelling was going away more each day. When they came to the boat, Rhett threw in Gaff's bucket and the boys pushed and pulled until the boat was in the inlet.

Both boys oared the vessel, although Gaff didn't feel he was doing his part. "You're paddling twice as hard as usual," he said, "and I'm paddling half as much."

Soon they were on the oyster banks looking for a place where the boat would be safe from the rising tide.

"Who's that?" Rhett noticed several people crabbing at their favorite spot and pointed.

Gaff squinted to see if he could figure out who was there. "I believe that's Ellen Marlboro and her gang from Clam Cove. Ellen's about as good at getting stone crabs as anybody I know."

"The day's calm. Not much wind," Rhett said. "The Clam Cove folks like to go crabbing on days like this." He maneuvered the bow of the boat toward a narrow stretch of sand where he believed the vessel would be safe. "Hey, Ellen," he called. "How did you get way over here?"

"We been walk and we been in the boat. Put food

and chillun in flat boat," she said, indicating a raft-like vessel lying on the oyster banks.

Rhett glanced at the children playing on the sandy road that meandered across the top of the oyster banks. "I hope you get a lot of stone crabs after that effort," he said.

"Mayham Heyward come too but he a-fishing in the surf." She glanced toward the ocean, where the man stood casting his line.

Gaff threw his bucket near some crab holes and he and Rhett secured the boat.

"Ellen, why're you always going crabbing?" Rhett asked.

"Gotta live, you know," she answered.

Gaff kneeled near a crab hole surrounded by a ring of mud filled with crushed seashells. "I betcha a biggie is propped up at the bottom of this hole."

Rhett eased his palm into the hole and yanked out a handful of mud that included a large stone crab. He pulled a rag from his pocket, wrapped it around the large claw and twisted the claw until it came loose. He dropped the claw into Gaff's bucket, then, with a flair of theatrical drama, he wound up his arm and twisted his body like a Major League baseball pitcher and threw the crab back into the water.

"That be a she crab or a he crab?" Ellen asked.

"I don't know. What's the difference?" Rhett asked.

"If a she, there be eggs under the shell. He crabs don' have eggs."

"I've never paid any attention to that," Gaff said.

"Iffen you put the eggs in the she crab soup the eggs'll turn the bisque pink, and it's a better quality stew," Ellen said. "Your ma knows all about that."

"I'm sure she does," Gaff agreed, "but that's one thing she forgot to tell me."

At that moment, Rhett let out a howl.

Gaff looked up to see his friend doubled over in pain. "Help, Ellen," he yelled. "The crab's claw has clamped down on Rhett's hand."

"Get Mayham!" Ellen screamed. "All you chillun up there in the road, get Mayham Heyward. He be a-fishing in the surf."

Two boys, one tall and the other small for his age, took off down the oyster banks for the flat boat. The larger boy extended his hand to the smaller one.

Oyster shells are sometimes as sharp as razor blades. After dragging the flatboat into the inlet, they paddled as though a monster was chasing them.

"I'm dying," Rhett groaned. "Just cut off my arm and let the crab have it."

"Just a little longer, Rhett," Gaff soothed. "Ellen's kids have gone for Mayham Heyward. He'll get you loose."

The small boy on the flat boat dropped his oar in the water. It disappeared under the boat. He leaned over the side and paddled with his hands.

"We're slowing down," the taller boy said.

"Keep going."

"We're slowing down," the older insisted.

"Beach the boat," the little boy said. "I can run and get Mayham faster than we can paddle."

"My legs are longer," the tall boy said. "I'll get Mayham."

Both children ran toward the sea. The tide was out and the beach looked a mile wide. A huge loggerhead turtle shell lay on the sand. The boys glanced at it as they passed. "Somebody cut the meat out," the smaller one said. "How wide you think that thing is?"

"Twenty inches if an inch."

"Can we take it home?"

"Not now. Gotta get Mayham. I see him. There, about a mile away."

"That's Mayham all right," the smaller boy said.

"The fog is coming in. Getting hard to see."

"Lead off," the taller boy called out.

The boys' feet fairly flew across the sand. They spotted the carcass of a shark in the billows.

"Don't even think about stopping to look," the smaller boy said. "Mayham!" he screamed.

Mayham Heyward turned. He saw the boy flailing his arms and put down his fishing pole and ran toward the boys.

"Rhett's hand is caught by a stone crab. Rhett Gingyard. He's about to die from pain. Come quick."

The three ran as fast as they could toward the crab holes. Along the way, they remembered other hands that had been captured by a stone crab. Some of the crabbers had died when the tide came in and covered them until they drowned. Others were left with broken fingers and cuts and bruises. They reached the sandy lane atop the oyster banks.

"Let the flatboat be," Mayham said. "We can make better time on the road." They moved along rapidly despite the hot sand, which had driven away other crabbers.

When they were within shouting distance of the group gathered around Rhett, the larger boy yelled, "We're coming."

Mayham surveyed the inlet as they ran. "The tide is rising," he noted.

The three made their way carefully down the oyster bank to where Rhett lay huddled over the crab hole.

"He must be turned," Mayham said.

"How?" Gaff asked.

"Let me talk to him." Mayham stooped down and put his mouth near Rhett's ear. "Is your arm twisted?"

"I . . . I don't know," Rhett moaned.

"Is your body uncomfortable?"

"I'm dying. All of me is uncomfortable."

"If I turn your body so that you're lying on your stomach, would that be better?" Mayham asked.

"Maybe."

"Take his legs," Mayham directed Gaff. "Hold them just as they are. Do not move them. I'm going to move his shoulder."

Rhett let out a scream.

"We have to move him to another position. I expect his fingers are broken and every movement will bring pain. But when he's been turned, he'll feel better. He's had some cuts from the oyster shells, and we have to be careful that he doesn't get more."

Gaff looked around. "Not a grain of sand. Not a blade of grass. Nothing but oyster shells all the way down to the inlet." While Gaff was wondering how turning Rhett's body would be possible, Mayham repositioned his friend's upper body until he was lying on his stomach and his arm hung in a natural position.

Ellen paced up and down the path at the top of the oyster bank, trying to determine how she might help. With no ideas in mind, she returned to where Rhett lay.

"I think we'd better decide what to do," Mayham said. "Everybody knows you can't force a stone crab to turn loose."

"Can we just pull out Rhett's arm and hand?" Gaff said.

"Lord no!" cried Rhett. "It's caught solid."

"The stone crab has spread out on the bottom, holding onto the hand, and he's bigger than the hole," Mayham explained. "We couldn't get him out if we tried."

Rhett began to tremble, nervous and tired. "Can I have a glass of water?"

Ellen ran to her canoe and returned with a glass of tea. She held it to Rhett's lips and he drank deeply. "I'm sleepy," he said.

"Don't sleep," Mayham cautioned. "We're going to get you out of here." A dog in the distance whined and howled as if aware of the dangerous situation on the oyster shells.

"What a perfect day!" Rhett wanted to burst into tears. "My hand is covered in blood. I can feel it."

The afternoon was already casting shadows over the scene.

"Is the tide coming in?" Rhett asked.

"Yes," Mayham answered frankly.

"What are we going to do?" Rhett asked, the crack in his voice showing his fear.

Mayham stood, his back to the crab hole, trying desperately to think of a solution. As he turned to face Rhett, nearly ready to collapse with fear himself, he saw Rhett's arm rising slowly from the hole.

Suddenly Rhett began to sob. His eyelids heavy with exhaustion, he finally said, "The crab released me. I'm free."

"Let's see your hand," Mayham directed.

Rhett's mouth opened wide in a grimace as he extended a trembling, bruised hand. The fingers were not broken.

"I died a death," Rhett said, "and for all the stone crabs we've taken, I have paid. The price was cruel and brutal."

Gaff kept a close eye on his friend as they walked home slowly together.

CHAPTER TWELVE

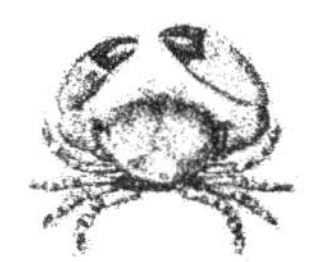

A Ghost of a Chance

It was on the day the first nip of fall touched the air that Mr. Gingyard announced he was going to the old mansion at Danseuse Drifts to check it out. The time was soon approaching when several Washington politicians would be staying at the ancient house behind the huge dunes known as "the Drifts." The house had no regular occupants and it was necessary to check on it now and then.

"Want to go?" he called to Rhett.

"Sure. Let's stop by and pick up Gaff."

As the pickup bumped along the rutted road, Mr. Gingyard asked Gaff if his leg had healed."

"Yes, sir," Gaff answered. "Good as new."

"How 'bout your hand, Rhett?"

"Not good as new, but better than it was when the crab clamped down on it."

"You understand that crabbing is off limits for a while," Mr. Gingyard said.

"Yes, sir."

Just then the pickup passed the spot where Gaff had been bitten by the copperhead. Gaff glanced at Rhett and both boys rolled their eyes. Neither spoke.

When they reached Clam Cove, the Cribbs were sitting on the porch of their small cabin. Mr. Gingyard pulled up in front and stopped the truck. "Everybody all right?" he called.

"Couldn't be better," Mr. Cribb said. He held up his leg, the one that had been swallowed by the alligator. "Almost lost this one. I'm wary of 'gator."

"Watch where you step," Mr. Gingyard cautioned as he drove off.

They passed the tiny church at Clam Cove, a place of worship where the community folks attended Sunday services.

"Dad, who's the preacher at Mount Moriah?" Rhett asked.

"I think Abraham takes care of that. They say he's right good, especially if you catch him when he's preaching about Moses leading the Israelites through the Red Sea. I hear the old man gets worked up when he tells that story."

"Can we come and hear him sometime?"

"Sure. We can come any time. If Mr. Blackhall's guests from Washington are at The Barony on a Sunday, he'll bring them over here for the service. They enjoy Abraham and get a kick out of his Red Sea story."

"I want to come too," Gaff said.

"We wouldn't think of coming without you," Mr. Gingyard said. The old mansion soon came into view.

"One thing we have to do is haul wood," Mr. Gingyard said. "The hunters will want a wood fire at night." He stopped the truck in front and they climbed out and walked inside.

"Ashes in the fireplace. I'll get the shovel out of the truck."

"I'll get it, Dad," Rhett offered.

"Not yet. Give your hand a little more time."

"We're pretty useless, with my leg and your hand," Gaff said to Rhett.

"Yeah. Dad says if you want to be a big boy you've got to play like them. Guess we're not quite ready."

Rhett and Gaff ventured upstairs and into some of the bedrooms. Everything looked clean enough but the beds had no sheets and pillows. When Mr. Gingyard came up, Rhett asked him if one of these bedrooms was where Miss Ginger Rogers slept when she came for a hunting party.

"Indeed it is." Mr. Gingyard walked to a window, pushed it up and looked out. "See that beach? That is where the famous Miss Rogers became so excited when she saw a flock of ducks she did cartwheels all the way down the beach."

"Did everyone laugh?" Gaff asked.

"I've heard it said that Mr. Alan Ladd laughed most of all," Mr. Gingyard answered. "He's also a famous actor from Hollywood, California, where Miss Rogers lives.

Gaff headed back downstairs.

"When are the people from Washington coming, Dad?" Rhett wanted to know.

"About ten days."

"Will they hunt ducks?"

"I expect they'll hunt duck and have a fox hunt or two."

"How about deer?" Rhett asked.

"There'll be a deer drive for sure."

"Will Miss Ginger Rogers try to kill a deer?"

"Miss Rogers certainly would kill a deer if she were here. She comes when Mr. Blackhall invites the society people, but when he invites the political folks from Washington, well, that's a different crowd. She won't be here, but I expect General Marshall to come."

"Great!" Rhett turned to leave the room.

"Rhett, guess what I've found!" Gaff called from downstairs.

"What?"

"A library. Come look. Every book you ever heard of is here."

"Did you know about the library?" Rhett asked his dad.

"Yes. It's a very special one."

Mr. Gingyard and Rhett walked downstairs. "It's a good one. Mr. Blackhall keeps all the Classics there, just in case his guests have time to read."

As they walked into the room, Mr. Gingyard

said, "Boys, there's something about this library you should know."

Gaff and Rhett stopped to listen.

"The guests report that something is watching over the books, and certain volumes are not to be read."

"How's that?" Gaff asked.

"I really don't know much about it—partly because I don't use the library, but mainly because I don't believe the story. Some people believe a supernatural phenomenon takes care of the library. It offers certain books to be read, and others are off limits. A spider's web covers the books that are not to be read, or so they say."

"You have to be kidding, Dad," Rhett said.

"Let's take a look," Mr. Gingyard answered.

They gazed at a set of Shakespeare, early editions, and the entire collection of Edgar Allen Poe tales. No spider web was seen.

"Dad, are you sure about the spider?" Rhett asked.

"I've never seen a spider in this library, but there is a kind in South Carolina that's very dangerous: the brown recluse. You never want to get a bite from that creature. You may use the books all you want, but should you see a spider's web, leave that book alone—not because of the old legend but because a spider can give a tortuous bite. I'm not superstitious in any respect, but the old story goes that should anyone see a spider's web attached to any book, that book should be left alone. I don't want a spider bite to be you boys' next big event."

The storied house had its signature, and the books on the library shelves seemed to be sensitive to southern culture. It was well known that families from the South Carolina Low Country had important libraries in their homes.

Rhett reached for a book that looked old enough to be the real thing: *Etiquette for Gentlemen.* "No book of etiquette for ladies?" he asked.

"Little girls were raised from the cradle to know the rules for ladies," Mr. Gingyard answered.

"Here's something interesting." Rhett pointed to a group of large volumes.

"What?" Gaff asked.

"All the books on this shelf are about medical treatment."

"Such as?" Gaff questioned.

"This one is *On the Chest.* Do you think that means the chest, as in where the lungs are, or could it mean a breakfront?"

"Where the lungs are," Mr. Gingyard said. "These old scaly books are about health matters."

"Here's one titled *Physiology, Therapeutics.* . . . This is spooky. I wonder why there are so many about health," Rhett wondered.

"Perhaps a physician worked here, or a nurse. Rumor has it, healing sessions took place in this room," Mr. Gingyard said.

"Healing sessions? What kind of healing sessions?" Rhett asked.

"Certain practices were believed to bring relief for ailments."

"Like what?"

"Like exercise for tired muscles, or deep breathing to aid the heart's rhythm."

"I don't get it." Rhett shook his head.

"Well, look at it this way: everybody was serious about the healing sessions. They believed the imagination of a boy is healthy and the same for a man. If a person could ease the cares of his heart and sleep, peace would come. To take it a step further, there is a story about the man who created this plantation—not the present owner, but one of his ancestors—that says he owned a large set of china, once belonging to a Russian tsar. The plantation master achieved a still and quiet conscience by gazing at the china in silence. It is said he spent entire days just sitting and looking at the plates, cups and saucers, and the like. The location of that china is a secret, but many people believe it is in this house. This much I know: there is a large vault room here. The door is thick and remains locked. For the life of me I cannot remember anyone ever going into the vault. Some folks think the story about the china is just a romantic idea, but I believe the china is in that vault."

"You don't *really* believe it, do you?" Rhett asked.

"Well, who knows?"

"Here's a book on the science and art of surgery," Gaff cut in. "It was published in Philadelphia in 1854."

"Oh, for heaven's sake," Rhett said. "Let's get away from this health stuff. If ever I decide to read one of these books, I believe it will be *Chemistry for Students*."

Mr. Gingyard left Gaff and Rhett to look through the many shelves while he continued his duties in the house.

Gaff gazed at the hundreds of other books and pulled one toward him. "*You Can't Go Home Again* by Thomas Wolfe." He thumbed through a few pages. "Listen to this: 'Down in the bowels of the earth there was a room where lights were burning and it was always night.' That sounds great. What do you think that room was?"

Rhett looked up from a book he was reading. "I don't know. Are you going to read the book?"

"Absolutely, but not now." Gaff pushed the book back into its slot on the shelf.

"Listen to this one." Rhett said. He read, "'Then she began looking about, and noticed that what could be seen from the old room was quite common and uninteresting, but that all the rest was as different as possible. For instance, the pictures on the wall next to the fire seemed to be all alive, and the very clock on the chimney-piece (you know you can only see the back of it in the looking-glass) had got the face of a little old man, and grinned at her.' "

"What book is that?"

Rhett looked at the book's cover and the first two pages. "The title is *Through the Looking Glass and What Alice Found There*. It was written by Lewis Carroll and published in Philadelphia by Henry Altemus."

"Is there a date in the book?"

"It has some handwriting on the first page that says, 'Presented to Curtis Dunn for best behavior and attendance at Sunday School by his teacher, Asa Stansell. December 24, 1899.' "

Gaff extended his hand toward *The Complete Short Stories of Guy de Maupassant*. He lifted the brown leather cover. "This book was copyrighted in 1903 and entered at Stationers Hall, London. I wonder what Stationers Hall was."

"I don't know. What's the name of the first story?" Rhett asked.

Gaff searched for the table of contents. "'Ball-of-Fat' and the second one is 'The Diamond Necklace.' The third is 'A Piece of String.' " He flipped to page 378. "I'm reading this one first: 'A Dead Woman's Secret.' " Suddenly Gaff put the book back, almost throwing it onto the library shelf.

"You can't treat old books that way," Rhett

scolded. "These books are valuable."

"I'm valuable too," Gaff said, his eyes wide. "A spider web covers pages 378 and 379."

That night, when Rhett sat with his parents in the living room of their home near the gate entrance to The Barony, he brought up the myth of the spider in the old library.

"First Timothy, chapter four, tells us not to spend time arguing over foolish ideas and myths and legends," Mr. Gingyard said. "I don't spend my time thinking on those old wives' tales. Every old house by the sea has its share of ghosts, but I would say you wouldn't stand a ghost of a chance of seeing one nor would you see a spider web on one of those books. If you do, just be careful that a spider doesn't bite you.

"We tell the guests in the old house at Danseuse Drifts the story about the spider web on certain books. They get a big kick out of the tale and spend many an evening talking about it. The thing that's important is this: it's no myth that brown recluse spiders are in the vicinity. If you are bitten by one, the skin near the bite dies and the victim experiences great pain. Such a bite takes months to heal. Be on the lookout for spiders and avoid them at all costs, but continue to enjoy the books in the old library."

"Gee, Dad, I'm glad to hear that. We saw some really good books there today. And we *did* see a spider web."

Avoid the book with the spider web until I can spray the library with bug killer and clean it up. After that, you can bring some books home. You might be surprised at how much you learn from them."

"I think I already know that, Dad."

CHAPTER THIRTEEN

The Atomic Bomb

From a secluded spot in a nearby woodland, Rhett and Gaff watched General Marshall arrive at the big house. Mr. Blackhall's long, black car pulled up to the mansion's veranda. The back door was opened and the honored guest left the car quickly.

The general walked erect, his muscles tight. His feet pointed straight ahead, each one placed directly in front of the other. His arms moved in rhythm with the swing of his legs. He walked with his usual pride but seemed preoccupied. Duke, Mr. Blackhall's chauffeur, unloaded the luggage and delivered it to the southeast corner bedroom on the second floor, which was dubbed General Marshall's room, to be unpacked. Within minutes, another car arrived with Senator Key and Dr. Spencer.

"I wonder which room they're all gathering in," Rhett said.

"Mama says they always get together in the sunroom," Gaff answered.

"You mean that big room with the curved wall of windows facing Winyah Bay?" Rhett asked.

"That's it. It's bright and sunny, and it's Mrs.

Blackhall's favorite. Mama said it's a cozy place for chatting, with huge, cushiony, flowered chairs of yellow and red and blue."

"Do we get to eat supper in the pantry and listen to the talk from the dining room?" Rhett asked. "I want to hear more about the atomic bomb."

"You and I will eat in the pantry tonight, and whatever is said in the dining room, we'll hear it. Mama will be busy with the guests, but she'll be sure to hear us and give us the big eye if we make any noise."

"I'm familiar with that look," Rhett admitted. "When she glares at you in silence, that's the worst."

As usual, Mrs. Dorn served Rhett and Gaff earlier than the Blackhalls' guests. The boys finished

their meal and sat quietly, listening as each guest was seated in the dining room.

"Senator Key, you may sit next to me," Mrs. Blackhall said. "And, Dr. Spencer, here, on my other side. My husband and General Marshall can sit opposite us."

"It is my pleasure to dine next to so elegant and intelligent a lady," Dr. Spencer said with a bow.

"What a nice thing to say," Mrs. Blackhall responded with a beautiful smile.

After some shuffling of chairs, all were seated.

"It is lovely weather, General," Mrs. Blackhall remarked.

"It is, indeed," Marshall answered. "Do you often ride through the woods and marshlands of The Barony?"

"Almost every evening, to get a little fresh air. The wild boar come, looking for roots and small ani-

mals, and it's a pleasure to watch them. I have an innate love of nature."

Soup was served first. Then, Francie Dorn carried a huge platter of rabbit to the table, followed by a variety of fresh steamed vegetables. An hour later, coffee and apple pie finished off the dinner.

As they all relaxed, satisfied after a filling, tasty meal, Mr. Blackhall brought up the subject of the atomic bomb. "Is the use of the bomb still in your jurisdiction?" he asked General Marshall.

"It is."

"I believe that civilization will be wiped out by it," Mr. Blackhall said.

"Is that so?" Dr. Spencer asked, a quizzical look on his face. He leaned toward his host.

"Indeed," Mr. Blackhall responded. "I believe that all will be destroyed by it."

"What do you think, Mr. Blackhall, of atomic energy?" Senator Key inquired.

"Phooey! It'll be no great boon. It's just a way to get around the inevitable."

"Rhett," Gaff whispered. "They're going to get into an argument."

"Sounds that way. Listen! Mrs. Blackhall's trying to hush them up."

". . . and I believe our future is not uniquely determined by the new phenomena," she was saying. "The external world has to be considered. As Tennyson said, 'God fulfils Himself in many ways.' "

"General Marshall, I visited the White House and talked with the president at length," Mr. Blackhall said emphatically. "If he has a solution to the matter, he didn't let me in on it. What do you think is going to happen?"

General Marshall asked for a refill of coffee and settled back into his chair. "There's an old story I heard long ago that comes to me in times of stress. I depend on it more than anyone would think. The glory of it is forever."

"What has your story to do with the atomic bomb?" Mr. Blackhall asked.

"Everything. Absolutely everything."

"I can hardly wait for the tale," Senator Key said.

"Pray continue," Dr. Spencer said. "Tell us the story. I have a strange feeling I will benefit from it."

"Do tell us the story, General," Mrs. Blackhall urged.

"If you insist, but you must keep in mind that this tale is my inspiration—not necessarily is it anyone else's. It fires me, impassions me, guides me. Perhaps the lesson I glean from the tale leads me to scorn dangers, in the likeness of John Barleycorn, but it is the grandest lesson and I have learned it thoroughly."

"Let us hear it," Mrs. Blackhall pleaded.

"It didn't start as a South Carolina Low Country story," the general explained, "but I've restructured it and made it my own fable. I'll roll back a century or so."

"Never was a story more enthusiastically awaited," Mr. Blackhall sputtered.

"Once upon a time," General Marshall began, "Carolina was owned by King George II of England who strutted his favorite courtiers to this country to operate it for him. He granted the lords proprietors—and that is precisely what they were, lords over the baronies and other estates such as this one—much leverage in running this country. They were the governors. But, alas, the peasants of England did not fare so well. For the slightest provocation, they were thrown into jail and sometimes lost their heads.

"One day three peasants were brought before the king. The first was thrown against the left side of the throne.

"'Of what is this man charged?' asked King George.

"'Your Excellency,' the guard said, bowing from the waist, 'this man is known to have acquired violins in order to take them to America and give the colonies the advantage of beautiful music. He has studied the wood, design, and acoustical physics. This man is familiar with Guildhall University faculty of arts. He will take away our culture.'

"'Take him to the Tower!' King George roared. 'Bring the next prisoner.'

"The guard threw the next prisoner to the right side of the throne.

"'Of what is this man charged?' asked the king.

"'Your Eminence, this man has been known to take some of the small mulberry trees to America with the intention of producing silk from the silk worms that make their home in mulberry trees. It is from our mulberry trees that we English obtain remedies for dropsy, dyspepsia, vertigo, and tumors.'

"'Take him to the Tower!' King George blared. 'I am ready for the next prisoner.'

"The guard pushed forth the last prisoner and threw him to the marble floor.

"'What did this man do?' King George asked.

"'Your Prominence, the elegant purple robe in which you are attired attained its exquisite hue from the indigo plant so prevalent in the American Low Country. This man has invaded the minds of the Americans with the idea of oppressing the English with a higher expenditure for the indigo plants, thus denying you and others of that most revered of colors.'

"'Take him to the Tower!' King George screamed.

"The man on the floor leaned up on an elbow. 'Your Eminence,' he said, 'I've noticed your dog, a Corgi.'

"'My dearest friend,' King George proclaimed. 'But why do you speak to me?'

"'If you would not send me to the Tower but give me one year to work with your dearest friend, at the end of that year I will have taught your Corgi to sing the most famous aria from an opera.'

"'You would teach my dog to sing?'

"'I promise.'

"'Guard!' King George screamed. 'Give this man a room near the kennels. Unchain him at once and see that he gets everything he needs.'

"As the guard took the man away, one of the other prisoners asked the unchained prisoner, 'Why did you do that? You have a year to worry. You know you cannot teach that Corgi to sing. Your death at the end of the year will be more torturous than mine.'

"The unchained prisoner said, 'At the end of the year, King George may be dead. I may be dead. The Corgi may be dead. Who knows what will happen before the end of the year? And by the way, do you know the most famous aria from an opera?'

"'No,' the prisoner replied.

"'I know it and it is just possible that I can teach that Corgi to sing it.'

"The first prisoner was then taken away, to the place of execution at the Tower.

"The end of the year came. King George and the prisoner who was working with his Corgi had become friends. The prisoner had been given the job of dog minder. Any fear of losing his life had faded. Indeed, he treaded with the potentate, attended parties, and had been given living quarters where the nightingale's song could be heard all day long.

"My behavior is based in this fable: when I am confronted by a dreadful situation, I will wait a year before making a decision. Many things can happen in twelve months. A year has not passed since President Truman gave me authority over the atomic bomb, but during the months that have passed, much has happened to ease my mind. I am fully convinced that by the end of the year I allotted to this situation, we will have fewer fears and other matters will demand our attention. We'll wonder why we got so worked up over the bomb."

"I'm not going to worry about the atomic bomb

anymore," Rhett whispered. "General Marshall is a smart man. When his year is up, we'll be thinking about our plans for all the things we want to do and the atomic bomb won't be a part of it."

Gaff nodded.

CHAPTER FOURTEEN

A Looming Threat

"Gaff, do you sometimes think we're being brought up in families that live shut off by themselves?" Rhett asked. "I mean, we don't see other families and visit anyone except our kinfolk and that's not very often."

"I think about it," Gaff admitted. "I also think about all the things we get to do that others know nothing about."

"Such as?"

"Well, we know there's a vessel or two on the ocean floor near us, and you said you saw gold there. Besides that, you and I get to go to the mansion and hear famous people talk and I don't know anyone else our age who does that."

"Yeah, I guess we're lucky," Rhett agreed. "We pretty much do what we like, as long as we don't raise suspicion. It won't be long before Dad will take us hunting with the important people who visit The Barony."

"Really?"

"Dad says we're almost old enough to hunt now. We'd have to be on our best behavior because he can't take a chance on us doing anything to upset the celebrities. But he wants us to become good hunters."

"Your dad is the dog minder and the horse minder and that's about the most important thing, at least to Mr. Blackhall," Gaff said.

"Dad said when General Marshall was here with Senator Key and Dr. Spencer, everybody killed a deer except Dr. Spencer. Dad says, being the doctor to the president of the United States and all, he may be the smartest man he knows, but he can't hit the side of a barn. Mr. Blackhall said he has some unfinished business about that."

"What is it?"

"I don't know. Something he's going to do about Dr. Spencer's shooting way off the mark. But he can't do it until Dr. Spencer comes back for another visit, and who knows when that will be? Dr. Spencer has to attend to the president and keep him in tiptop shape, and that keeps him busy. "

"I don't know what Mr. Blackhall could do about Dr. Spencer's bad shooting," Gaff said.

"I don't know either, and I'm not going to worry about that. I'm going to give it a year. By then we won't care." Both boys laughed.

"I'm glad you haven't forgotten that I saw that gold where the blockade runner lies at the bottom of the water," Rhett said.

"I wouldn't forget that. Suppose the gold will always be there."

"I don't know about that. We should give some thought to obtaining some of the treasure, don't you think?"

"Maybe," Gaff answered warily. "It's a dangerous place and too far down to go without some equipment, which we don't have."

"Shoot. We can't wait on equipment. I'm going down." Rhett said.

"Rhett, it's dangerous. Both of us have had plenty of injuries this year and our parents would pitch a hissy fit."

"They don't know about the gold." Rhett raised his hand. "See. My hand's nearly healed. It won't be long before I can go crabbing again and that's just as risky as going down for the gold."

"Your dad will never allow you to go crabbing again," Gaff said.

"I'll convince him when the time is right. I know what went wrong. I was reckless. Took my mind off the game. That won't happen again," Rhett answered. "I'm going crabbing soon. And I'm also going down and have a look around the old blockade runner. You can go with me or not."

"Oh, I'll go."

"When?"

"When what?"

"When will we go to the bottom to look around the ship?" Rhett asked. "You don't have to go if you don't want."

"You're not going without me. I want my half of the gold. How much gold is there?" Gaff wondered.

Rhett thought about the brilliant gold bar he had seen. There had to be more. "Well, I don't think we'll bring up enough to make us rich, but I want at least a few pieces, just to keep."

"You think we'll get to keep it?"

"Well, it all depends on our parents, I guess. Your dad's the game warden and he has certain responsibilities. My dad's the superintendent and he's supposed to let Mr. Blackhall in on everything that happens at The Barony. Somebody's bound to call the Charleston Museum, and there goes our gold."

"What if we don't tell?" Gaff asked.

"A story like that would burn a hole in my chest, and yours."

A worried look crossed Gaff's face. "We might go to jail for hoarding Confederate gold."

"I don't know about going to jail," Rhett said, "but I'll tell you something: when I get the gold and hide it some place where I know it'll be safe, I'm going to give myself a year. By the time the year is up some treasure hunters may have found the gold and we'll know if it's safe to keep it or not. During that year Mr. Blackhall might sell The Barony and the new owners won't let us live here, and we'll just take our gold wherever we go. And who knows, during that year the old law about finders/keepers might be enacted and the gold will belong to us. One way or another, I believe that at the end of the year we'll be safe and happy with our gold."

Gaff clapped his hands. "When do we go for the gold?"

"As soon as we can get back to the library at Danseuse Drifts. I saw an old book about treasure hunting in the library and I've got to get my hands on it," Rhett said.

"We'll both read it," Gaff said.

That night, Rhett asked his dad about the book on treasure hunting.

"Don't depend upon finding treasure and getting a fortune for nothing," Mr. Gingyard said. "How many people do you know have found a treasure chest, or whatever? None, to be sure. One has to prepare himself for the future—study, set goals, work hard, and when one reaches his goals, that's the treasure. People don't get something for nothing. Get the idea of finding hidden treasure out of your head. Don't set your mind on finding a fortune. That happens only in fiction—*Treasure Island*, maybe, but not South Carolina." He shook his head. "What a waste, to put your hope in finding treasure."

Rhett couldn't understand why the subject of treasure hunting put his dad in such a dither. He had already found the treasure. All he had to do was figure out a way to get his hands on it. "I'm sure you're right, Dad," he said, agreeing with his father to avoid a quarrel that might lead to suspicion. "Now that I think about it, I don't want to read that book in the library."

Late one afternoon the following week, a procession of fishing smack from Clam Cove followed each other in single file to the estuary. Rhett and Gaff tagged along. It was a ragtag army that sought a good meal from the incoming tide. They stopped at the first bridge they came to, baited their hooks, and leaned against the railings to wait for a nibble on the line. A girl named Daisy caught the first bass.

"Anybody know anything about sunken ships?" Rhett asked.

A man who was straightening out his tangled line said, "There're some blockade runners on the ocean bottom. That makes for good fishing."

"Anybody find anything from a blockade runner?" Gaff asked. "Any . . . uh . . . treasure?"

No one answered.

"These people don't know anything about finding something of value," Rhett whispered to Gaff.

"Aunt Ida found some gold," Zachie said offhandedly. "Up 'til the day she passed on she always claim it was gold."

Rhett's countenance changed. "Did you see it?"

"It was right smart shiny. Aunt Ida kept it wrapped in a handkerchief, in a drawer."

"Where did she find it?" Rhett asked.

"Don't know that anybody ever asked her 'bout that."

"You sure?" Gaff asked.

"That gold went to the grave with Aunt Ida. Fune'al man put it in her pocket. Say somethin' 'bout 'lay up for yourselves treasures in heaven.' That's all I know 'bout that."

Gaff and Rhett eyed each other.

When the two boys arrived at Rhett's house, Mr. Gingyard had news.

"I met some folks this morning. I was doing a little work on one of Mr. Blackhall's boats, *The Tide's Up*, and a family idled their vessel to a stop and asked directions to the Intracoastal Waterway."

"They were practically there," Rhett said.

"I directed them to the Waterway, but we had a

right interesting conversation. They're from Montreal and spend a lot of time on their boat. I believe they know what they're doing and seem especially knowledgeable about weather patterns."

"How's that, Dad?" Rhett asked.

"The pilot, the father of two children, said he and his wife noticed a fragment of clouds southwest of Long Island in the Bahamas. They think it's a tropical depression and it's building. He got in touch with the weather people in Miami and they told him that conditions are a little tricky but they're ripe for the storm to gain strength. You boys ready for a hurricane?"

"I remember the last one," Rhett answered. "We were invited to ride it out in the big house. Dad, you had a lot of work to do afterward."

"We were at the big house too," Gaff said.

"Have you told Mr. Blackhall?" Rhett asked.

"No," Mr. Gingyard said. "I'll tell him this afternoon. He's asked me to take him for a tour of the waterfront portion of the The Barony. You know how he is. About every other month he wants to take a look at his land from the water and see if everything is stable."

Rhett looked perplexed. "That'll be a long ride."

"It'll take a while," his father answered. "But it's a good idea to check on the waterfront now and then."

CHAPTER FIFTEEN

Going for the Gold

There was no sense of panic at The Barony. No windows were shuttered, and whatever feeling of fear existed was tinged with ignorance of the immense power a hurricane packed. The storm, a whirlwind that could whisk Elijah away, sighted for The Barony, tore into the inlet where the blockade runners had gone down, and grew stronger before it turned north.

The Gingyard family hurriedly moved into the big house, taking the second-floor corner room—General Marshall's. The Dorn family, also on the second floor, was about halfway down the hall. The Dorns had been allowed to bring Daffy Deer with them. He slept on a handcrafted rug between the beds.

"This is a cozy set-up," Gaff said.

"Don't get a thing such as that on your mind," Mr. Dorn said. "No hurricane is cozy. We're fortunate to have the Blackhalls take such good care of us. Others on the estate are fending for themselves."

Francie Dorn knew more about the food in the house than Mrs. Blackhall, and she took it upon herself to serve the meals at the dining room table. Rhett and Gaff talked seashells. They had heard rumors of huge shells washing ashore during hurricanes, and several monstrous ones were in the sunroom to show for it.

The wind and rain continued into the night. Mr. Blackhall made the best of it, offering food and drink and trying with all his might to get a clear message from the radio. Finally the wind abated, but the rain held steady. Although Rhett and Gaff felt a burning desire to get to the ocean as soon as the weather cleared, they were constantly reminded that their assistance would be needed in clearing the land of fallen trees and limbs.

Next morning, Mr. Dorn and Mr. Gingyard went out to survey the damage. Together, in an old truck, they toured the property as best they could, dodging fallen trees. When they came back, they reported that all people were safe but there was much property damage. Weeks of work would be spent in clean up and restoration. Almost every inch of the land bore scars. Huge live oak trees were down; debris was everywhere. A headline in a Charleston newpaper the next day would read, "The Whole State Was Scared."

The southern heat had no compassion for area inhabitants. The sun beat down mercilessly on the rooftops by day and the soaking night rains gave little much-needed relief. Swamps and ditches were littered with carcasses of wild boars and cows. A deer, still alive, hung high in a live oak tree. The Gingyards and Dorns moved back into their homes.

The hurricane damage to The Barony kept Mr. Gingyard and Mr. Dorn busy and they had little time to supervise their sons. Rhett finally convinced his father that such a storm comes maybe once in a lifetime and it was important that he look for anything the storm brought from the sea. "I'll spend the next three years doing show and tell," he said. His father was convinced. The boys were free, more or less, to do as they pleased.

A couple days after the storm, Rhett fixed his glowing eyes on Gaff and asked, "Just tell me, are you game enough to go down for the gold?"

"Are you?" Gaff countered.

"You betcha," Rhett said. "Our dads are so busy with all the work the hurricane left for them they won't be paying attention to us."

The boys set out for the burial site of the blockade runners.

"I've never seen so much seaweed," Rhett said, surveying the marshes. An area that had been half-water and half-land two days ago was now all land, covered with every kind of debris. "There're barrels of stuff, everywhere."

"And there *are* huge shells." Gaff slapped his hands together. "I see a monster of a Florida Fighting Conch, as sure as my name is Gaffney."

"Get your mind off shells. We're going for gold. Exactly where was I when I went down? We've got to find the exact spot."

When they reached the inlet, they secured their small boat and found the walkway on the crown of the oyster banks. The boys picked their way around fallen trees, trash, and scraps of mystery items and looked toward the ocean, but they couldn't see it.

"Where in the heck is the entrance of the inlet from the ocean?" Rhett asked.

"It's gone," Gaff said.

"That's where the blockade runners went down and that's where the gold is. That place doesn't exist anymore. The storm surge washed the entrance to the inlet away."

Suddenly the sun came from behind a cloud, and all about them glistened.

"That's an omen," said Gaff. "We'll find gold today. Everything is all silence and glow.

"You don't know what you're talking about," Rhett scowled. "The surge of the sea came onto the land right here in this inlet, and it changed things. We're not actually at the place we think we are."

"Things *don't* look right," Gaff agreed.

"They're not right," Rhett shot back. "We'll find no gold today and never will again."

The boys walked around, looking. "See that pile of seaweed and trash over there?" Rhett pointed. "That's where I went down, I'm sure of it. That was the entrance to the inlet. That's where the storm roared in from the Atlantic and ruined everything."

Gaff saw a mound of sand and suggested they take a load off for a while and gather their wits. They stretched out on top of the sand and watched the clouds pass.

Rhett was addled and couldn't bring the exact layout of the area to mind. "Where will we hide the gold when we find it?" he asked.

"I don't know. Where are things usually hidden?"

"Dogs bury their bones in hideaways," Rhett said.

"Squirrels dig holes in the ground for their acorns," Gaff reminded.

"What about the graveyard?" Rhett asked.

"The graveyard at Mount Moriah?"

"Is there another?"

"No, but a graveyard is for dead bodies," Gaff pointed out. "I know some of the people buried there. There are some crosses, and a monument or two. And there are people who believe that if an item used by the dead person during their lifetime is placed upon the grave, the spirit of the deceased will not come back to haunt anyone. Every kind of item you can think of is on those graves."

"True," agreed Rhett. "I've seen eyeglasses, drinking glasses, bottles of medicine, all sorts of things over there."

"Would you want your gold to be in a place like that?" Gaff asked.

"Yes, especially because no person would think to look there for it. It's the graveyard. People don't hang out there. They go there for rest, or some people like to experience sadness over a loved one, but they are not looking for treasure. Our gold would be safe in the graveyard."

"Where would you put it?" Gaff asked.

"There's a monument of wood. It's carved with the man's name and the lightning that took his life. The lightning is nothing like a flash but a zig-zag bolt. The bolt starts at the top right corner of the marker and ends at the man's name. He probably was stricken in the heart. We'd never forget where the gold is if we dug under the bolt of lightning and buried it there."

Gaff thought about it. "A graveyard. I just never thought of that kind of place."

"What sort of place did you have in mind?"

"Well, some place in the attic, or in the woodhouse."

"Your father goes to the woodhouse every day

in winter. He would find it." Rhett said. "There is no place as safe as the cemetery. Besides that, every available man is busy with saws, cutting the trees that blew down in the storm. The Mount Moriah area is a place where we would never be discovered. No one's working on that part of the estate."

"I think you're right," Gaff agreed. "We'll dig a hole under the marker with the bolt of lightning and we could never forget where that place is."

"But we're not going to get our gold," Rhett said in misery. "That place has washed away. What else can we do? . . . Wait a minute. I'm getting an idea. . . . I know. We'll collect seashells. I've already noticed some excellent turban shells, sundials, trumpets, wendletraps, and about every class of clam. We'll have the best shell collection in the state."

"From gold to seashells," Gaff droned. "That's a comedown."

"Can't win 'em all." Rhett stood and began to wander around.

Gaff made his way toward a large pile of debris that had washed in.

"Rhett!" he yelled. "Come here! You won't believe this!"

"What is it?" Rhett called out.

"Gold! Look!"

Rhett flew to Gaff and zeroed in on a shiny object. It *was* gold. No question about it. "The ocean washed it up," Rhett said. "We didn't have to risk our lives and dive for it. It just came right here to us. I can't believe it."

Gaff picked up the shiny bar. "There's writing on it. It says, 'Confederate Gold—1862'. It's the real thing, all right." He slipped it into his pocket.

Rhett poked around in another pile of trash. "Here are two more!" he yelled. "Come see."

Three gold bars were more than they had expected to find had they gone to the site of the shipwreck. They continued to look among the shells and debris but found no more gold.

The boys were tired and went back to their resting place on the sand mound. Lying there, they could hardly take it in.

"Gaff?"

"Yeah?"

"I think we'd better go bury our gold and say nothing to anyone about it. What do you say?"

"Good idea. Let's not push our luck."

"Yeah, easy does it," agreed Rhett.

The boys backtracked until they were nearly home, then took a path through the woods to Mount Moriah Church. They entered the cemetery, not with the usual joy that one would expect of two boys who had discovered gold but with a kind of sadness. They meandered along the alleys of gravestones and talked about the bodies at rest there and the generations of families that had populated Clam Cove. Mount Moriah wasn't a museum like the cathedrals and burial places in large cities. It was a small, plain place in the woods on the coast of South Carolina. Finally they came upon the marker with the bolt of lightning.

"I think this is a good place to hide the gold," Gaff declared. "There's no room here for another burial or grave to be dug. Some of the nearest graves display items used in life by the dead deceased. There's a drinking glass, and on the next grave is a spoon. The families of the people buried here believe these items are sacred. If anyone messes around with them, the spirit of the dead deceased will come back and take revenge. People won't be poking around at this place."

"Exactly," Rhett agreed. "You think it'll be all right if we dig a hole under the lightning marker? Do you 'spose any spirit will get revenge?"

"Heck no. Nobody comes around here anyway. If they did, they'd be scared to touch anything. This is the safest place in the world to hide something. What are we going to wrap the gold in?" Gaff asked, changing the subject

Rhett dug into his pockets and came up with a handkerchief. "A handkerchief seems to be the proper wrapping for gold," he said.

With their hands, Rhett and Gaff dug a deep hole under the wooden marker, placed their gold there, covered the treasure with dirt, and spread leaves and pine needles over it.

“Not a soul would ever think anyone had violated this gravesite,” Rhett said.

“Nobody in this world,” Gaff agreed.

“You know,” Rhett said, “we have to have a kind of gentleman’s agreement that neither of us will ever mention the gold again for a year.”

Gaff held out his hand. “For a year. I give you my word. Not only will I not mention the gold, I’ll try to forget it for twelve months.”

Rhett grabbed Gaff’s hand. “For a year. We don’t know what the situation will be at the end of the year. We may decide to go back and search for more gold. Or we may decide to let things be. General Marshall said that after a year has passed, many problems will have been solved and most questions answered. We’ll give it a year.”

The boys shook hands and went home.

THE END

The Ghost of the Crab Boy

from *Coastal Ghosts* by Nancy Rhyne © 1989
published by Sandlapper Publishing Co., Inc.

The Ghost of the Crab Boy

Bryan came to the marsh (he called it the creek) at what is today Huntington Beach State Park to catch stone crabs for his family and for friends like Miss Addie McIntyre. Stewed crab was a staple in his diet, and he believed crabmeat had a restorative effect for one who was ill.

"The house we stay in be a two-room house with one of these end chimneys, and it be over there cross the King's Road on Miss Addie McIntyre place. She been sick in bed for four weeks, but she mendin some now. She been mighty low. She feed on crabs what I bring her from the creek, and sometimes it help a little bit, but not too much."

There are about a thousand different kinds of crabs, but the stone crab is noted as the best tasting of the crabs that are consumed. It is a crustacean and lives within a hard shell. The body is broad and more or less flattened, and the five pairs of walking legs are jointed. As if that were not enough, the stone crab has snapping claws that are exceptionally strong. This story of Bryan is justifiable proof of the power of the claws of a stone crab.

Stone crabs live in holes they hollow in the marsh mud. Those who look for these crabs can immediately identify their holes. As they burrow into the mud on the bank of the marsh when the tide is low, they throw up behind them seashells and debris that had been deposited there by rising tides. Each stone crab's hole is encircled in a mixture of shells and mud.

Bryan could spot a stone crab's hole quicker than a

bullet could hit its mark. I mean, he'd just reach right down into the hole and pull out the crab, and he acquired a surefire technique of getting the crab without the crab snapping his fingers.

"The crab holes," he once explained, "been same long as my arm. I worked my hand down the hole slow and, when I feel like I be gettin near the crab, I dig my fingers down in the mud. Then I yank out a passel of mud, and the crab be in that mud. I always go in the hole that way and get what I want. It not be too much trouble. Most people use a long wire with a hook on the end, but that be a pack of foolishness. I just reach in and get 'em."

After filling his bucket, Bryan would go home and pick the meat out of the body and claws. His mother really knew how to stew crabs. She'd put the crabmeat into the stewpot and add a little pepper and salt and a mite of nutmeg. Then she'd add the yolks of two broken-up eggs, some crumbled-up biscuit, and a spoonful of vinegar. While the crabs were stewing, she'd make a pan of fresh biscuits that were just right for sopping. Man, when you sopped those biscuits in the stewed crabs, now that was real eating!

One evening Bryan came to the marsh and extended his arm into a crab hole. It was getting late, and he didn't use his usual precaution in taking the crab. Suddenly, the claws of the crab clamped down on Bryan's middle finger and nearbout cut it off. But the crab held on. Bryan let out a holler that was heard nearly to his home across the King's Road. He flailed around in the air, jumping, screaming, yelling, but the crab would not let go. The old crab just clamped his claws tighter. Bryan, his whole arm down in the hole, pictured the crab, his eyes on their short stalks, looking amused at *his* catch.

After a while, Bryan got tired and he couldn't scream

quite so loudly. His yells became more of a mournful wail than a shrill cry, and his face lay on the marsh mud. By this time it was getting late, really late, and although Bryan told himself there was nothing to worry about, he knew in his heart of hearts it would take a world of luck to save him. The tide would be coming in soon, and, unless the crab turned him loose, the tide would rise over his body. When the tide went back out, he'd be nothing more than a limp corpse. Or maybe a stiff one. He didn't know which.

Bryan continued to wail, but no person heard him. A creeping chill began to possess him, and he peered over the marsh to the trees. He could see a lamp in a cottage in the trees. Everything was quiet except for the incoming surf. Even the dogs were quiet. Not one howled. It came to Bryan's mind that no one was going to save him. And the crab never once lightened its grip on the boy's finger.

A grim sense of blackness, and the hopelessness of fate, seized the soul of the weary boy gripped in the tongs of the crab's claws. Bryan had gotten himself into trouble, and there was downright nothing he could do in self-defense. What have I done? he asked himself. How did I get into this mess? His voice was little more than a squeak, small and thin, but still human. "Help me. For God's sake, help me." As the tide came closer, he thought that if the rising water took his life, God would take him to the land of Canaan where he and Joshua were having a happy time.

The tide came in, then went back out. Daylight came. That was when the body of Bryan was found. He was taken to Heaven's Gate Church, and a funeral was held. Bryan was buried at the edge of the marsh where high-tide waters would cover his grave, since the family superstition ruled that the sea must again receive its own dead or it would claim a new victim.

One night after all the chores were done around the seaside homes, a thunderstorm rolled in. Black clouds skudded just overhead, and rolling thunder shook the earth. Moss hanging from the live oaks blew every which way, and rain came in sheets. In all of this, a voice was heard: "Help me. For God's sake, help me." It was believed to be the voice of Bryan.

If you walk the beach at Huntington Beach State Park, and dark clouds come in from the sea, and the color of the ocean changes from blue to gray, and the surface of the water turns choppy, and the soft warm air turns chill, listen. You may hear the voice of Bryan. It's during the storms on that beach that he comes back, still begging someone to release him from the claws of the stone crab.

Author Nancy Rhyne enjoying life on the Carolina coast.

About the Author:

North Carolina native NANCY RHYNE has spent most of her adult life in the South Carolina Low Country. She and her husband and sidekick, Sid, have traveled thousands of miles of backroads over the years, gathering folklore and building a treasury of oral southern history. Nancy has also spent decades researching regional and national archives, particularly the WPA narratives. Her stories are testimony to her love for the southern landscape, southern people, and southern traditions and lore. Nancy now lives in Columbia, where she is a frequent visitor at the South Caroliniana Library on the University of South Carolina campus. She claims *The Crab Boys* will be her final book and she and Sid will enjoy a quieter retirement. But, as Nancy's popularity continues to grow, it's unlikely she'll be able to follow through on this decision.

Other Books by Nancy Rhyne:

Alice Flagg: The Ghost of the Hermitage
Carolina Seashells
Chronicles of the South Carolina Sea Islands
Coastal Ghosts
The Jack-O'-Lantern Ghost
John Henry Rutledge: The Ghost of Hampton Plantation
Low Country Voices
More Tales of the South Carolina Low Country
Murder in the Carolinas
Once Upon a Time on a Plantation
Plantation Tales
Slave Ghost Stories
The South Carolina Lizard Man
Southern Recipes and Legends
Tales of the South Carolina Low Country
Touring Coastal Georgia Backroads
Touring Coastal South Carolina Backroads
Voices of Carolina Slave Children